1

Publisher: Published! A Village Voices Affiliate
Copyright 2012 by Blue Canyon

ISBN-13: 978-0-984682775
ISBN-10: 0984682775

Manufactured in the United States

Publisher's note:
Blue Canyon first came onto the scene of writing erotic
fiction in the anthology – The Cougar Book, published
by Logical-Lust Publications in 2010.
Edited by Jolie du Pré, the book quickly became a
major hit among readers of erotica.
Available at all fine book-selling establishments.

Songs in the Key of Goth

Book II

I would like to thank the many women I've known in my life, for teaching me how to love and how to make love. To them I owe a debt of gratitude that transcends the mere moment of orgasm. To them I owe the teachings of near-spiritual elevation.

Oh God! Oh God! I'm…

World of Pain

By:
Blue Canyon

The lone motorcyclist rode into town on the roar of his V-twin engine. He pulled up in front of a store and parked the bike, looking more like a cowboy tying his horse to the post outside a saloon.

He had a look about him. Not exactly handsome, but striking and intense. Angular, chiseled features made women swoon for him. He stood well over six foot and weighed-in at just about 220, maybe a little less. Muscular—yet on the slender side—his jeans fit snuggly to his legs and ass.

More than one pair of eyes watched as he lifted one of those legs up and over the motorcycle and swung it around to the ground. They were all trying *not* to watch. One such pair of eyes did not belong to a Miss Molly Gerkin, from the Gerkin ranch just east of town.

Molly, it seemed, had come into town simply to buy supplies. She was not looking for any 'male' involvement. She was already involved with a man, the owner of the hardware store. He was busy arguing with her about the things she wanted to buy.

"Molly, Molly. If it were up to me, you know I would let you buy the stuff. Your credit came back denied. There's nothing I can do."

"My credit is better than most people's around here and you know it, Mr. Barker. You are denying me because of that shit—Tanner."

"Molly, you know Mr. Tanner has nothing to do with the credit reporting agency."

"Mr. Barker, you are not a nice man. You would let my ranch go to ruin before you would sell me supplies?"

"I don't make the rules, Molly."

"No, Tanner does. You just follow him."

"Now that's a pretty strong accusation. You shouldn't say things like that. I'm not trying to treat you bad."

"It sure sounds like it from here."

They both turned to the odd, silky voice that spoke to them. The first thing Molly noticed was his dark blue shirt. It not only went well with his jeans, but contrasted perfectly with his well-tanned skin. She thought he looked gorgeous.

He carried the few things in his hands he'd come to purchase. He approached the counter and set them down next to Molly's and looked the man in the eye with a stare that could make a statue blink first.

"I'll take these."

The man behind the counter moved nervously. He began to obediently scan the items, but he never stopped staring at the stranger and making sure he didn't move too quickly. The first thought travelling through his mind was not the gun that fit so perfectly on the wall right next to the register just out of customer sight, but rather of how much hiding room he'd have underneath that counter should he need to duck.

"And these," he added, pulling Molly's things closer to his and the register.

"Mister, you don't want to get involved in that. You'd best leave it alone and ride out of town." It was the first sign of back bone the shopkeeper showed.

The stranger didn't intimidate easily. He leaned forward at the waist which just brought his face closer to Barker's. He said nothing, only staring deeper into the man as if that were enough. But it was enough. The shopkeeper sheepishly reached out and began scanning the items Molly Gerkin had put up there.

The stranger paid properly with cash, Mr. Barker looked at it as if he'd never seen money before. The stranger grabbed the things and left, leaving Molly to stand there, looking back and forth from his back to the shopkeeper. Finally, just about the time the front door closed behind the stranger, she managed to unglue her feet and made her way quickly to the door. Without so much as a wave or a glance backward, she went out.

"Hey, wait a minute."

"Which car is yours, Miss," he said, realizing she'd finally caught up. "I'll put these in it for you."

"Who are you?"

"I'm just a guy who's passing through."

"You got a name?"

"Clint."

"Clint? Sure, why not. Clint, what?" She had a sinking feeling she knew how he would answer.

He sighed.

"Clinton Theodore Sterling, Ma'am."

Not the answer she expected, at all. Backing up a bit to stare at him, Molly smiled but, to her credit, did not laugh, although she felt inclined to. Instead, her finger poked out in the direction of the El Camino parked right in front of the store. He walked over to it and set the bags with her things in the back.

"What brings you to this town, Mr. Sterling?"

"Please, call me Clint."

"Okay. Clint."

"I'm here to see a man."

"Oh?"

"Hank Tanner."

Molly backed up again and looked like she would run for her car and leave as quickly as she could. But she hesitated.

"What do you want him for?" The way she said *him* made it sound like a curse word.

"He's not a very nice man."

"And you want to see him. Does that mean you are not a very nice man?"

"I do not intend to be friends with him, Ma'am."

"Please, call me Molly," she added, her voice softer than before.

"Molly," he said, smiling. "That's nice."

She smiled more warmly.

"Thanks."

"As I said, I'm not here to make friends with the man, if you know what I mean, Molly. But as to whether or not I am a nice man…well, I may be, but then again, there are those who might dispute it. I can't really say."

Somehow, Molly felt more comforted by his words. He was not here to be friends with Tanner. Someone once said: *the enemy of my enemy is my friend.* To this day she cannot tell you why she said what she said next.

"Do you have a place to stay?"

"No, Ma'am. But the night will be clear," he said, looking up at the afternoon sky.

"There's no need of that. Stay at my place. I have room."

"I wouldn't want to intrude."

"I have lots of room and I live alone."

"Wouldn't you be afraid?"

"I already am, every day."

"Excuse me?" Clint looked surprised.

"What could you do to me Tanner hasn't already threatened?"

"I see." Then he thought about it for a moment. "Lead the way?"

She smiled again and sat down in her car while he mounted his motorcycle and kicked it in the balls until it roared with power. He followed her through some turns and down a dirt portion of road, finally reaching her ranch. It looked a lot like a ranch, a simple, though large house surrounded by fields for miles with fences dissecting throughout. Some horses grazed in the distance.

"Very nice, Miss."

"Molly."

"Yes, of course. I'm sorry."

As they walked in, she showed him briefly around.

"That is the bathroom if you need to freshen up. Also, if you like, you can take a hot bath and I can wash your clothes for you." She looked into his sparkling eyes.

He stared at her as he had the shop keeper, but it felt differently to her. Somehow he seemed not only to be looking into her soul, but he was communicating with her on that level. She felt overwhelmed with an urge to wrap her arms around him and…

She quickly pushed the idea out of her head. It had been too long since she'd been with a man and she was being just a little too eager for modesty's sake.

"That sounds wonderful, Molly. But, may I ask, what is that wonderful smell?"

"Oh, I'm so sorry. I've forgotten my manners. That's dinner. It'll be ready soon. Are you hungry?"

"Yes, I am. Thank you."

"Good. I've been told I'm a good cook. It will be nice to have someone else appreciate my food for a change."

"If you don't mind my asking," he spoke to her back as she retreated to the kitchen, "why aren't you married?"

She turned and looked at him with a stare that asked why he would want to know such a thing. She decided he was just being curious and neighborly. So she chose to answer honestly.

"He died."

"I never understood why, but people believe it appropriate at times like this to say 'I'm sorry'."

"It confuses me, too. But thanks for the sentiment. It was a long time ago. I'm over it...sort of."

"Is it something you prefer to not talk about?"

"Yes it is."

"Then we won't talk about it. You run this place by yourself?"

"I have a hired boy. He comes after school to take care of the horses. His family went on vacation to Florida so he won't be around until next week."

"Okay," he said as he sat down to eat. She placed a plate in front of him and he ate as if he hadn't in days. Afterward he sat back and rubbed his muscular chest and firm belly. "That was perhaps the best meal I've ever tasted."

"I wouldn't go that far, Clint."

"I would. I don't come from a long line of good cooks," he joked.

"I'm glad you liked it."

They stood and he stepped over to her. He raised his hand to her arm in a simple friendly gesture but she stiffened and held her breath. He mistook her action for fear.

"I won't hurt you, Molly."

"I know."

"Would you mind if I took that hot bath now?"

"Be my guest. I usually run out of hot water before it's full, so I'll just put the pan on the stove. It gives me just enough to top it off and make it feel comfortable."

"Thank you very much," he smiled.

When she brought in the water, he had already gotten his shirt off and she could see the rippled muscles in his stomach. She tried not to stare. This was going to be a difficult night.

She poured in the water and left quickly as he wasn't stopping at the shirt. She didn't know if he would undress completely in front of her, but she knew she had to leave the room before he went any further.

After a while, as she walked through the house, she passed in front of the bathroom. The stranger hadn't bothered to close the door. He was out of the tub and beginning to dry off. He saw her and dropped the towel and stared at her. She could do nothing but stare...at his penis.

He invited her with his unabashed gaze. She stepped forward as if someone were manipulating her with a remote control. His eyes never left hers and hers never left his cock. He made no move to stop her or suggest he didn't want her. In fact, he was beginning to rise to the occasion.

She wasn't sure she believed it, but she thought he might be as interested in her as she was in him. Could that be? She felt like she'd gotten so much older since Frank died. No man called on her and she felt unattractive.

But she kept walking. When she got close enough, she reached out a hand. It came in contact with his leg just to the right of his testicles and she caught her breath again, like she had in the kitchen earlier.

It had been a long time since she was with a man. Emotion and lust overcame her. She made no effort at modesty as she touched him in intimate ways like a familiar lover. His body gave her feelings she wasn't sure she *ever* had even back when her husband lived.

He too, came willingly, placing his rough hands on the tender flesh of her breasts. She moaned with pleasure. The pain hurt and she wanted more. When his hands slid down her back she felt a shiver surround her body like another skin.

He seduced her completely, either because he had talent or because she desired it. She didn't really care which. She needed him inside her and she was going to have it, and he seemed willing.

Their lovemaking lasted well into the night and Molly deeply breathed in the scent of sex that filled her room. He didn't have the finesse as he pounded into her gracelessly, but her pleasure increased with each thrust.

They rolled together in sweat, seeking a solace which could be achieved no other way. A smile consumed her face and she lay peacefully, enjoying the memories playing over and over inside her head. But sadness overshadowed her bliss.

She looked deeply into his eyes and saw more lust within. But no matter how deep she looked or which way she searched, she could not see him staying with her for long.

After a time, she let go of the sensation that coursed through her and relaxed into sleep with her head resting in the crook of his armpit. The lingering odors of soap and sex wafted into her senses as consciousness fully escaped her.

The morning rose in the east and the sun broke through her eyelids disturbing her perfect slumber and dreams of clover and butterflies...and sex. She came back to consciousness reluctantly, fighting to remain in her fantasy realm and the bliss within.

But the sun had become unrelenting as it burned through her sleep, rising up to a perfect height to shine through her window and directly onto her face. She lazily pushed back the covers and exposed her naked form. She hadn't slept in the nude since she was married. She looked down at herself and, for the first time in a very long time, admired what she saw.

It was not vanity, but rather that he'd enjoyed her so well. He found her so attractive. He hadn't kept his hands off her. He desired her and devoured her. She felt like a queen.

Molly felt she could float on the fluffy clouds that danced around the blue sky. Then she looked over to the other side of her bed. Her *empty* bed. Had he left so soon? She *knew* he wouldn't stay, but why did he have to leave so soon? Something inside told her she would *never* know the answer.

†

He parked the motorcycle on the side of the road more than a mile away from the ranch. The noise would attract too much attention and stealth could still be on his side. He walked the rest of the way in the trees for cover, but no traffic rode by and he was not seen.

The edge of the trees lined the ranch in a smooth circle, but it looked like an acre of open land between that line and the main building which was his goal. He would wait until nightfall, even though it appeared abandoned.

†

Darkness could be a double-edged weapon. While he could maneuver with less chance of being seen, the likelihood of him being surprised by a guard or an alarm greatly increased. He took great care to look out for traps and trip wires.

Once inside, there was a greater chance of setting off some alarm. However, that no longer concerned him. Inside was...well, inside. He surveyed the well-adorned home and decided which way would be most likely to hold his quarry.

Clint Sterling crouched behind a china cabinet as the man walked by. The bulge in his jacket under his arm was evident. As soon as the man went past and his back was turned, Clint jumped out from his hiding place.

The guard went down without a sound. Clint slid through a doorway and came face-to-face with the only other guard that seemed to be on the premises.

The man drew his gun, pointing it expertly at Clint's chest.

"Who are you?"

Sterling considered his many answer options. There would be no stopping his bullet and any answer would more likely aggravate the situation. So, he decided to carry on the great American tradition, he'd learned from some of history's greatest heroes.

He fainted.

The man with the gun approached quickly, abandoning any safe distance considerations. Clint Sterling moved quickly. His hand shot up and deflected the barrel of the gun enough for his other hand, equipped with a sharp object mostly resembling an ice pick, to find its mark. The man went down in a pool of his own blood.

Standing over the body but looking around the home, the stranger finally moved toward the stairs leading upward. The bedrooms would be up there. With any luck, the owner of the house would still be asleep. Clint had come to see that he slept for a *very* long time.

Walking up the stairs quietly, hands once again empty, he saw the man approach from a distance of several meters. There was no cover, no stealth, no way to avoid a direct confrontation.

"Who?"

"Sterling."

"I don't know you."

"No. No way you could."

"Then..." the man looked around, "...why?"

"Because it must be."

A moment of silence passed between them. The other man seemed to be trying to absorb what he'd heard. Or perhaps, Clint thought, he was just assessing his situation and creating a strategy. Maybe he just wanted to run.

"Well, my name is Tanner. I'm afraid, my friend, I am not as informidable as my so-called *guards*."

There were no more words to be said. The two warriors crouched and parlayed, evaluating each other, guessing strengths and, more importantly, weaknesses. Neither made an aggressive move...at first. Both chose to assess the other for a time.

Then, inevitably, a hand struck out, and it began. Both men trained in martial arts-like styles, simply grabbed each other, attempting to throw the other to the floor. This would certainly gain one the advantage, but both being more or less equally matched, accomplished very little by what they were doing.

Also inevitable, though, was a change. Tanner feigned a stumble to his right and brought his left hand up to strike, hoping his entire body weight would go into the punch. It did. However, Sterling managed to dodge by less than a quarter inch.

Swinging full around, Clint brought his open hand down onto the other man's shoulder. The chop had the desired effect. Tanner fell to one knee. He

21

swung his arm up to block the expected blow, but it did not come.

Sterling, anticipating Tanner's anticipation, swung his knee up into Tanner's face. The man went down as blood dripped from his nose. He struggled to focus his eyes but the broken nose wouldn't allow it.

Suddenly Tanner became very calm as if finding his center. He found his way to his feet and turned warily toward even the slightest sound from Sterling's feet. The stranger made a move to test Tanner's focus. The man reacted quickly and accurately.

Once again the two men danced—one seeing and one sensing on another level. The loss of sight didn't slow Tanner down by much. He lunged forward to connect with the other man. The stranger spun like a ballerina and reached out, grabbing a sword from the wall in one graceful move.

Without losing his momentum or his near-perfect arc, he unsheathed the sword and buried it to the hilt in the chest of the homeowner. Tanner went down, gasping as if trying to maintain the life that waned from his damaged body. Sterling stared deeply into the dying man's eyes and watched as the life force drained away like a feather in a gale.

"So," Clinton Theodore Sterling spoke softly, intimately, "you're the man causing all the trouble in this town. A pleasure to meet you."

The other man fell in a heap at the stranger's feet.

†

The lone motorcyclist rode across the desert where no road had ever been, enjoying the roar of his V-twin engine between his muscular legs. He rubbed slightly at his neck and then flipped a switch on his motorcycle between his 'fat-bob' gas tanks.

"I have made first contact. There will be no problem making them think we are friendly."

He reached for his neck again and pulled. The synthetic mask came off his head easily, revealing his grotesque alien features. His smile would scare the skin off a grand master martial artist.

"The baby I gave her will look like one of them."

The Rock

By:
Blue Canyon

And suddenly darkness fell. I looked hard but could see nothing. When I took one tentative step forward, I finally saw something. Stars. My chin connected with something very hard and pain shot up my leg, jerking me to an instant stop. It must have been short because I'd put my hands out in front of me—waving them about maniacally—and never felt a warning.

The thunderous roar from moments ago had ceased, replaced by random coughs and some weak moaning. Somewhere in the distance a woman sobbed. To my right I saw a flash from an electrical short—perhaps a bare wire hanging down. I could hear and feel the electricity in the air as it buzzed against a table top. Then all went black again. With people milling about aimlessly, that electrical wire could be very dangerous.

A part of me wanted to laugh. Danger, it seems, had found us without our wandering around searching for it. Still unsure what happened, I squatted to my hands and knees and began to slowly make my way toward the nearest voice. It called out for help but had no strength—as if the life had been taken out of it already. Yet it called.

At one point the electricity shot through the air again and I saw the wire, now merely three feet away from me. I began to question my sanity. Moving around, even in a crouched position as I was, could prove dangerous—even fatal. But the voice called on. So did others.

27

In the complete darkness, I tried to keep the image of the wire to my right—hoping to move past. Then it crossed my mind there could be other wires hanging—waiting to give their deadly gift to anyone foolish enough to get near.

I found a wooden table leg and swept back and forth in front of me. This made crawling more difficult. I felt like a three-legged dog, trying to move and maintain my balance, all at once. A table bumped into me and I went down, injuring my left shoulder. I'd probably have a nasty bruise on my upper arm. Of course, in this light, who would notice.

I worked at this facility for six months and no one noticed me anyway. But getting noticed wasn't why I came to work here, nor was it the reason for my earning a degree in microbiotics. I specialized in micro-computerization because I wanted to build the first nano-bots. I'm not sure, but I don't think I need a man to do that.

And yet I've felt so isolated. No one has spoken to me. I'm not just the new kid on the block, I'm the new kid with pimples. Some days loneliness overwhelms me and I cry. Somehow I've always managed to keep it in until I get home.

I worked with some of the greatest minds in the country, and at least two or three sexy men. But because I'm a young woman in a man's world, it leaves me being the outcast. And at only twenty-two, there's still so far to travel.

But I got lucky and landed this job with a research facility with a reputation for being cutting edge. Although, looking around the room at what little I can see right now, I don't feel so lucky.

My best guess is a cave-in. I didn't know these places even had underground levels before I was hired on. But this place had been here for years. Why there should be such a disaster now—I didn't know. Although we weren't doing anything with the military, perhaps some radical group decided we're a threat and planted a bomb. Buried down here in complete darkness, blinded by bursts of electrical light, there's no way to know what's really happened.

Then my hand touched something with hair. I jerked as I heard another groan. A voice came to me, weakened and odd, somehow. Something I couldn't explain rode those sound waves to my ears. An emptiness, or a lack of energy, perhaps—something beyond my words to describe.

"Help me."

"I'm here," I replied, trying to sound confident.

"W-Who?"

"It's Arianna Long. I'm the new girl." Even after six months I remained the 'new' girl. I would probably be the new girl five years from now.

"Ah, the pretty one, with the great body."

He noticed? Someone—anyone noticed? I thought they were all just scoffing at me, laughing at the newbie. Someone once gave such people a pretty name to take away some of the hurt. Intern. That was my title. No matter my field of expertise or the lab they assigned me to, I was just 'the intern'. It sounded like some old television show. I tried not to chuckle. Under the circumstances, it didn't seem appropriate.

"Thank you," was all I could think of to say.

"Can you lean a little closer so I can see you?"

I leaned down but could see only a rough outline, the darkness made any real clarity impossible. I quickly noticed something to my right. Lights had begun to flicker. I thought the wire might be chasing me. Apparently the emergency backup generator had kicked in. Fluorescent tubes began winking on—one after another.

Soon the light overhead flashed on and I caught my breath short. A boulder the size of my car lay on the body of the man I'd been talking to, crushing him from the chest down. I looked at his face—pleasant and handsome, though weak and pallid—he smiled.

His rich blue eyes set under dark curly hair. His striking nose with just a hint of a slalom hump came to a tip that pointed at me—following me when I moved. I offered him a smile in return, churning it up from the depths of the manners I'd learned as a child. The man's life was over. No medical team could save him even if they arrived at that moment. All I could do was keep him comfortable and happy.

"I've seen you around. What's your name?"

"I'm Doctor Shetzer." I guess he saw my face fall just a bit. "Brian," he added.

I smiled. "Well Brian, I've seen you around. What do you do?"

"Microbiotics."

"Oh yeah? Me too. Too bad we didn't get to work together."

"That's not likely to happen now," he groaned.

"Oh, come on," I lied as best I could. "You're just going to need some time to recover."

"Listen, honey," pain twisted his voice into a raspy saw blade. "I know what the score is."

"You do? Who is winning?" I tried to sound jovial.

Brian sagged. I felt terrible. When he didn't speak, I tried to move our conversation forward.

"You..." I began strong but wasn't sure how to continue. "You should try to keep a positive attitude." I was surprised to hear my voice sound firmer than I felt.

"Listen, Arianna—is it? I know the end is near."

I couldn't find my voice. Even if I could stop choking, I didn't have the words. I sat back to ease the pain in my legs, staring into his sad and sexy eyes. Taking a couple deep breaths I leaned an arm against the same block of wood Brian's head lay on. I got real close to his face so he could talk softly and not strain so much to make his voice carry. I rested my head on my arm.

"What can I do to help, Brian?"

"I don't have much longer. I can feel it."

31

"I know," was all I could manage.

"I want..."

I held my breath. My breathing had become so loud in my head I didn't want to drown him out.

"Do you believe in granting a dying man's request?"

"If I can," I replied, looking at the huge rock and hoping he didn't ask for me to pull him out, or something impossible like that.

"I...I want to see your tits."

"I..." my voice trailed off as I tried to find the right response. I scanned the room to see how many people would be close enough to overhear. "Are you kidding?" I looked down at my chest. Small bumps dented my shirt and I wondered how he'd even noticed I had any.

"Please?"

I wanted to say no but my hands came up to my shirt like they'd already decided. I couldn't be sure how best to let them out and still cover myself quickly if someone noticed. My button-up shirt was no longer tucked into my pants and I figured just lifting it up would be easiest.

So I grabbed the shirt at the bottom cuff, snaked my hands up to get my fingers under the bra, and pulled both hands to my chin. Both Brian's hands were free and he moved one over with a jerky motion and touched me. My nipples were hard, either from a chill, an odd kind of excitement, his intimate touch, or the fear of getting caught.

32

I watched around the room, allowing him to continue touching me while I scanned for observers, until I felt his hand fall away. When I looked back, I saw his eyes had dropped a couple inches toward the floor and they looked a little glazed over. I slowly lowered my shirt back over my breasts.

I leaned over and kissed him on the forehead. "I hope it was good for you."

A Name by Any Other Rose

By:
Blue Canyon

'Twas merely lust filling her inside, like a dark hand of animal desire wrapped around her heart. Her black soul wanting only the satisfaction of the flesh, her eyes wandering from one male to the next, the wanton woman sank to depths no fallen angel would dare.

Her mind twisted by her constant need, she continually sought only the physical gratification that sated her for barely a moment and then she would, as so many times before, return to the hunt. And one man after another would willingly yield, succumbing to her wiles.

She was born, Rose Antonia Riley Ford, from a prosperous family with some standing in the small community from whence she sprang. But prosperity and affluence held little meaning for a girl led not by her head—nay, not even her heart could be a true guide when lust bloomed from the depths of her tender body.

The better part of her youthful life spent in the futile search for more gratifying moments, she had now come to an impasse. She took the time, on occasion between her hunts, to ponder the meaning. She derived many conclusions, but for lack of any true guidance, settled on none.

And so, over time, her heart grew heavy with confusion and longing. She searched high and low for a nobler purpose to life, nary missing an opportunity to stop and devour some unsuspecting, yet willing young man—more out of need for blind fulfillment now than any real desire to continue her whorish ways.

Despite the urges that welled within her and would oft times drive her to the brink of insanity, the still-young woman would sometimes be struck full on by the remorse that often accompanies such a lifestyle. And her heart would, once again be rent with the pain and regret brought about by a budding conscience.

Verily, a young maid such as she could torture herself into an asylum with such dire contradictions of thought. And she found herself, when not on the prowl for the next sampling of fleshly delights, seeking more a solace than an understanding which continually evaded. She clung to any unmovable object that would support her through these tribulations.

One such object was Wilford Denton Hemmingforth, an Earl by his own claim, though none could prove his lineage. People, it seemed, dared not question his self-proclaimed title. In less than a year after his peculiar arrival, he declared himself magistrate, in a town that, heretofore, had none. And naught but a fortnight passed when the town was christened with its new name:

Hemmingforth.

Rose met Wilford quite by happenstance one sunny afternoon when the sky was filled with spritely birdsong that soon faded beneath the more prominent music from a different source. She searched, more in the open than she should, for satiation and momentary bliss, once again. Many prospects strolled out on such a day and her eyes made attempt at every pair that passed. To her dismay, none willingly returned her gaze.

Wilford, quite to the contrary, set about in a more dutiful capacity. Madame Chatterwell's boarding house was known to accommodate discrete liaisons and he and two other gentlemen marched in that direction with official papers to cease and desist.

The impromptu town council voted to eradicate all such undesirable elements from their Christian community in an ill-fated effort to extricate the seductive lure of the evil one that still managed to live among them, despite the town's innocent Christian beginnings. This, apparently, would be the first step in ensuring the purity of growth among the town dwellers. And Wilford, quite intent on his quest, never met Rose's gaze, even at a passing glance.

Nevertheless, Rose found herself inexorably drawn to the stalwart figure. Her footing faltered as she continued to watch the man—not where she trod—and she nearly stumbled into the abattoir. Her lust suddenly abated for reasons she could not fathom, she strode for the safety of home with many a confusing thought mulling through her head, drowning out the song that had begun in her heart—too far away to hear, too deep-rooted to ignore.

The two of them were heterogeneous, to be sure, despite her heritage. She certainly could not approach such a man with her desire unchecked. Should he see her with lust unfettered, he would surely hand her directly to the Abbess, and Rose would forever be without the warmth of a man's touch.

However, her desire remained checked at that very moment—tethered by an invisible rein. After some pondering, she came to realize she desired this man on a more spiritual level, although she could hardly be called upon as knowledgeable about such matters. She sought his companionship, his *favor*, perhaps, but not to seduce him. Though surely she could not soon understand why—nor, perhaps, ever.

Yet she knew him not. And would not until she gained control of her urges. His office held him far too busy for socializing and her stature surely lay beneath him. Rose knew this without anyone telling. *A true and intelligent person knows who and what they are. And one should always stand in the appropriate company. The crossing of such social barriers is considered ill-mannered and morally unacceptable.*

But as her thoughts became more focused on the magistrate and less on her own needs, she knew she would eventually have to cross those lines or forever live in despair and emptiness. This, more than any other thought, gave her pause to consider the choices she had made throughout her nearly twenty years. She felt as an old maid, for her toils had been fruitless and trivial and weighed heavily on her soul. If only she could bury her past and become a lady once more.

Would that there could be a way to purge not only the desires but the stains left from past indiscretions. She would keep her head high as people pointed, saying: Behold! There passes the lady Rose, Duchess of Hemmingforth, heir to the Ford fortune, wife of the Magistrate. None would dare say such things in her current state.

The weeks that followed proved to be the most torturous for Rose. Her heart longed for the security of truly knowing a man and being with him in all senses. However, as time passed in the manner it often did, and she'd only caught glimpses of him around town during the course of his duties, she began to feel daunted.

Sadness would not pass through her unaccompanied. It haunted her along with many other feelings, all vying for her attentions, all crying to be dealt with first. A myriad of erratic thoughts and feelings bombarded her at any given moment, giving her pause. There was no study she could partake, no council she could seek, no trust to which she could cling. Rose had never felt so solitary.

On one particularly glorious day in early summer, Rose felt like dancing. Her gait bounced as if to invisible music and her smile—perpetual. Her feet tapped to the spirited rhythm of a heartbeat. Life felt like fresh spring.

However, on this most conspicuous day, Rose had deeper reasons for a joyous demeanor and a pert glow. For truly, on such an auspicious occasion, her feet strode not to the beat of her own heart, but of his.

The moment had come and it was to be today. She walked in a bee-line toward the office of the magistrate where her appointment would be met by the figure occupying all her dreams of late.

Although her joy may have been premature as she was not going to meet for any social reasons or even a precursor to courtship. Nay, this day she would become the new secretary for the office, thus giving her both a place of respect and a proximity to Wilford Denton Hemmingforth.

Wrong though it may have been for her to have such thoughts; her mind put their names together in whimsical images of marriage. Rose Riley Antonia Hemmingforth, many would think it sinful to speak those names aloud in this manner.

Even so, her mind sang the names. She could see them in writing, though she dare not put pen to paper for fear of being overseen. As her hand touched the door of the highest office in the township, the image of writing shattered away as might a tea cup dropped. Her heart felt as if it would burst with anticipation.

Public offices demanded no knock and she entered with only the slightest of hesitations. Once inside, she stood immobile as she absorbed her surroundings. Surroundings of the like she'd never beheld.

Ornate could be considered self-gratifying and sacrilegious and yet intricate carvings and delicate scroll-work decorated the majority of furnishings. The magistrate, himself, sat behind a desk larger than any Rose had ever laid eyes upon. She felt diminished, overshadowed by its enormity.

With light sparse and furnishings heavy, the room gave the appearance more of storage than function, though Rose found the fragrance much less distasteful. Being of small stature herself, she felt intimidation from every direction and cowered from imagined overbearing. But was it *entirely* imagined?

The magistrate stood and peered down at her with enigmatic eyes. For the moment she felt a pang of guilt, as if she were of criminal background and he the acting judge. His voice came as thunder yet she felt soothed in a way she could not easily put to words.

"Is there some service this office can perform for you, Miss...uh?"

Try as she might, Rose could keep the quiver from her voice only in the intent. The sound that came out, despite her best efforts to the contrary, shook delicately—meekly. It sounded like fear, though she should feel none. This disturbed her sereneness and faltered her resolve.

"I am Rose Antonia Riley Ford. I have been appointed to the post of secretary to the magistrate, good sir," she spoke as she curtseyed. "Be that the title given you?" she asked, though she knew it to be so. She struggled to keep her eyes from meeting his as so many men had done to her in the past. Hers was not humble obedience but fright. Fear of being caught with a lustful thought in her head. Although such urges were abated…mostly, she felt them close by—never far from her—and feared their sudden and unpredicted return

"I am he."

In all things, Rose knew she must remain lady-like and proper. She felt she should look chaste and mannered, knowing her place. She must present the *new* her, despite the *old* feelings that rose within to belie and unravel her resolve.

Rose decided the turmoil inside her young mind must be like unto the feeling of a child when approaching a new horse. The beauty of the majestic beast lured while the sinewy musculature frightened, telling of its strength, and only a narrow tether held it abay.

The magistrate must surely have seen the struggle taking place within her very eyes, for as he descended toward her, he too took on a new expression. His—one of concern, perhaps even pity, a little too fatherly, he hurried to her side.

"Truly, why have you come, my child?"

"'Twould please me greatly to work for the office of the magistrate, your honor."

"My dear, there is no need to address me in such form. I am not an officer of the high court. Nor am I royalty."

"I would be remiss to allow my manners to falter, sir. I've been taught well how to address my betters."

"My dear, the brilliance of the very sun shines from your lovely smile, whilst I am but a humble shadow," he said, bowing formally.

"Oh, sir," she fluttered. "You do me too much honor. I assure you, I am not worthy."

"My dear young maiden, have I not seen you noticing me as we passed in the street? Several have been the times when the smile glimpsed from the corner of my eye has turned an otherwise dreadful day into complete joy."

Rose's cheeks flared with shame even as the sweetest smile spread from the corners of her mouth. The syrupy sounds that flowed as he spake made her head swim in wonderful images of hope and happiness. With some effort she looked up and...met his gaze.

"What would be the appropriate manner to address you, my lord?" she mouthed in bold tones.

"I should think 'Mr. Hemmingforth' would be an acceptable method of address. And if not offended, I shall henceforth refer to you as 'Miss Ford'."

"It would be an honor, sir...I mean, Mr. Hemmingforth." Now she fluttered all over. Dark desires and wholesome happiness fought with each other—mortal enemies—a battle perhaps of the ages, and it took place in all corners of her heart.

"Then come, Miss Ford, attend me. This," he pointed at a prominent desk, smaller than his and yet larger still than any she'd ever seen, "shall be where you will carry out your daily tasks. And may I say this room could not be lovelier."

"Thank you, Mr. Hemmingforth. May I inquire about the ornature?"

"A bit too much, perhaps?" his question given the semblance of rudeness by the aversion of his eyes as he surveyed the room. "And myself, no antiquist."

"It does appear a trifle vain, if you don't mind my saying so, sir."

"The truth is," he spoke quieter now, "some years ago I worked for the office of taxation and supplication. There was a man of some prominence in town who had a stroke of ill fate.

"He'd been tilling the soil in preparation for the next planting season and he struck open a vein of crude. Needless to say, it laid waste his entire crop before it could ever be planted."

"Ooh, the poor man," Rose offered compassionately.

"Yes. To make matters worse, not six months later I per chance found myself to be strolling through the office of patents, as I had business there, and overheard a rather zealous young lad carrying on about how he'd come up with a use for the vile substance."

"Indeed?"

"Well the prominent man could not pay his taxes. The rules are very rigid, leaving no margin for sentiment. Foreclosure was imminent, but he was not to be beaten."

"He created this beautiful woodwork?" Rose asked.

"He most certainly did. He labored for months. With no crop there was naught for him to do otherwise. So you see, my dear Miss Ford, I do not keep them," he pointed at his furnishings as he spoke, "out of vanity. The pride of having known such a talented man is my only sin. Touching the hand of a man so blessed by God creates a value to me that no monies could purchase."

"That is a fascinating story, Mr. Hemmingforth. It was very generous of you to offer that pour soul another means by which to keep his home."

"Generosity had little to do with it. In my humble opinion, his work is worth far more than money owed."

"You could have returned them."

Hemmingforth seemed hurt, as if he'd been asked to hand off his favorite pipe to a passerby on the street.

"I don't know that I have the heart to part with them. It would be akin to giving away a family heirloom."

Rose remembered a time of lost innocence in her own life—a time she'd given away something precious—a family heirloom, of sorts, lost, never to be returned. A touch of sadness crept into her smile.

Rose lived and studied and played in that town as a child until the summer after passing her seventeenth birthday when she happened upon a scene of such surprise and distaste that she could not avert her eyes.

Strolling aimlessly toward the small river that provided drinking water for the town, Rose hardly noticed any particular detail. She sought only an afternoon unfettered by obligations—not to mention the sound of horses which she found unpleasant—and to enjoy the beauties of nature.

As the trees yielded and she passed back into the sunlight near the banks, she could hear the babbling water and smell the fish and mud—though less pleasant than the smell of horses, she always felt calm when near the river. She just stood and admired the area as she often did, but when she looked toward the North, she saw.

Blinking several times to wipe out the image, she was afforded a full view of them. A boy she knew but not by name lay on top of Cynthia Greenwold, a girl from Rose's class. Neither wore a stitch of clothing.

The most interesting things were happening and Rose studied intently. Driven by budding forces she did not understand, she lost track of time. Her eyes glazed as she became unaware of her surroundings. When she found her sight once again she discovered the two had gone and her hands were buried under her own ankle-length dress. She was exposed.

Embarrassment swept in quickly and she dropped the hem of her dress down appropriately, looking around for witnesses. Her maiden purity remained untarnished by any eyes she could see. Accepting her good fortune, Rose returned to her home and the innocence of her family.

But the day after the next, whilst walking to the general store with vegetables from her garden to trade, a boy approached. He spoke in mannered tones...at first.

"Good day," his voice almost sang.

"And a fine day it is," Rose replied with a slight curtsey.

"I've seen you about, Miss—"

"Ford," she answered curtly. "And I would say you have. After all, I live here."

"Do you often walk by the river?"

His words struck her as a hand and she started, blinking back the beginnings of tears. Would that she could be sure he hadn't seen her base act, but some intuition told her he was about to reveal he had. A flush came to her cheeks and she lowered her eyes.

In that moment, he knew. Perhaps he had before, but now he was assured, convinced further by her expressions of guilt before even being confronted.

She had spoken her words of confession without muttering a sound. No doubt the town leaders would be proud of her confessions.

"Perhaps we could walk together," he said with abominableness.

"But I know not even your name, good sir."

"Tim Henning, at your service. A pleasure to meet you." He bowed accordingly.

"'Twould be inappropriate for us to be seen."

"Then we shall not be seen."

And then, rather suddenly, some sparkle in his eyes became apparent to her. She recognized him as the boy from the river before. Rose chastised herself for not seeing it when he'd first approached her. He'd been with Cynthia Greenwold on that day. Now, she too was convinced this young man had seen her own sinful actions. Her face flushed further but her curiosity swelled.

Thoughts of abjuration swept through her mind and she trembled. Her vows to the church would be for naught and her soul would be cast out. Confused, driven both by morals and desires alike, her feet chose for her. She made way in a different direction, leaving the boy without so much as a by-your-leave, though it be away from her chosen path.

The young Mr. Henning, not so easily put aside, accosted her once again, on a later day—this time managing to find her near the river. She'd come to ponder the thoughts he had first planted within her that now raged like a wildfire.

Morality, a subject always so crisp and simple, confused the maiden and she muttered to none but herself as a feeble woman near death. She spoke to no one yet sound escaped her lips. One might have thought her possessed, had they happened upon her as Tim Henning did.

He did not think her possessed or feeble. He thought her beautiful and approached in quiet. His hands were on her before she was aware of his presence. She struggled in reaction but soon succumbed to the touch of his manly strength. He touched her in ways not appropriate—sinful. And Rose found herself enjoying the warmth he ignited within her.

Time became as a blur, much the same way it had the day she'd seen him with Cynthia. Only glimpses of consciousness washed through her mind. They came in waves. At one point, her clothes had been removed. She became completely seduced by black desires and he amorally led her to further depths with the touch of his fingers—and his lips.

His weight on her gave her a feeling of safety, and even the pain of him stabbing her in that manner offered some strange comfort. Deep inside she longed for the moment not to end. This, more than any other thing, convinced her what they were doing was evil. And she definitely would not stop.

It took little time for Rose to master the simple skills required of her. At the end of three months, the Magistrate granted her charge over the entire office leaving him to matters of greater import as his position demanded.

Any person or home with so much as a rumor of un-Godliness would be called before him to answer charges of heresy or worse. And while Rose felt uneasy about the heavy sweep of righteousness that rolled over the town and risked washing away all remnants thereof, it had gone well into removing all evidence of evil as it intended.

She remembered her and poor Tim had coupled several times before the unfortunate accident with the new stallion his father bought. He'd not been an evil boy and Rose felt something akin to love for his show of intimacy. She later found that most girls fell in love with their first, only most waited until marriage before engaging in such physical couplings.

Sometimes tears would come, but they would be short lived as a boy walked by and drew her attention away from the painful memories. She would concern over a lack of conscience, and then a new boy would be on her—and in her. In those younger days, it happened often.

In Rose's life, distractions came easily. Despite her deep concern for the survival of the town, one late summer day Rose found reason to put aside her thoughts for sake of new ones. Wilford offered her thoughts that would occupy her mind for many nights to come.

"Miss Ford?" Wilford called on an early Friday afternoon.

"Mr. Hemmingforth, you startled me. I did not hear you enter."

"Forgive me. I…"

For the first time since she laid eyes on him, Wilford faltered. He seemed not to know how to proceed.

"Is there anything wrong, sir?"

"Wrong?"

"Has my work dissatisfied you in some way?"

"No. Certainly not. However, I wonder if you would be so kind as to attend Sunday meeting with me."

Rose's heart did a summersault. She fought to suppress her joy so her answer would sound calm. She felt no need to consider the offer, she knew her answer, and yet she hesitated. At times like these, control could be so elusive. Finally, she turned.

"I would be honored, Mr. Hemmingforth."

"Good." He too breathed a sigh of relief. 'Then it's settled."

Rose enjoyed the way her life began to unfold. First came the Sunday meeting. After which she accepted every opportunity to spend time with him. *Perhaps before long*, she hoped, *he will brave an announcement of our courtship.* It would come as no surprise to the townspeople who all had eyes.

Within her heart Rose could still, on occasion, hear the call of black desire sweeping over her soul like a cloud blocking the sun. Sometimes these moments were quite overwhelming. However, fortune had graced her—she'd endured most of these in private. After a time, and some embarrassment, she'd learned several methods of self-satisfaction. These would abate the call, if only for a short time. And although the scent that remained on her fingers allured, it did little to keep hidden her true nature.

The strongest power to help overcome that call was her proximity with Wilford. His strength, his heart, his voice—all were strong medicines in fighting the disease that churned within her most distant recesses. And she longed to eradicate it, to rid herself of its vile presence. She listened to the melody of his words at every opportunity.

No doctor could help but perhaps God had shown her a path to salvation. She felt compelled to walk it as narrowly as possible for surely there would be no alternate route. All other roads led away and she would forever be damned. Eternity did not frighten Rose but eternal damnation should not be sought by anyone believing of God, not as long as she still had the will to choose and the strength to govern her emotions—if only a little.

Rose felt assured, as days became cooler and were called weeks, there would be no evil dare set roots in Hemmingforth. As it surely had become a town where the sun shone always and God Himself came to rest from fighting the evils that lay elsewhere.

Let it not be said there is no evil one but only blackness within a person's heart. For verily, on that day late in November as everyone prepared for their feast of giving thanks, an evil greater than any known in the little town had taken notice of the war waged against it and the losses incurred.

On a dark night, as temperatures dropped in foretelling of a strong winter, the evil one sent a messenger to the unwary town. Not one to be known outright, he sent a messenger not of savagery but of subterfuge.

His messenger arrived only two nights after the feast had passed and people still hid from the gluttony of which they'd partaken. The messenger, as with all sent by the dark lord, did not announce itself, rather taking quiet root, seeking out the softer soil to push through.

It could smell the weakness, the desire, in a person's heart, even from great distance. Drawn to it as a moth, it gradually swept through the town, searching each person one by one until that bitter-cold night a week before the celebration of the birth of Christ, when

55

it discovered the heart of Rose Riley Antonia Ford and the darkness that lay buried deep—yet remained.

The beast's messenger drew to it, swam in it, savored the taste as one might a fine wine. The messenger wrapped one soft, warm hand around Rose's heart and massaged lovingly. The other hand swept to her pudendum. The messenger rubbed vigorously but with great focus. Rose hugged her pillow tightly remaining asleep yet disturbed out of any *real* rest. When she awoke between dampened sheets she felt irritable and knew not why. Nocturnal emissions were an embarrassment and she scorned the hands that betrayed her steadfast effort to remain on the path.

Somewhere in the bowels of the earth the messenger sat in darkness, smiling. The heart it found that night would make a wonderful home. It could dwell there for eternity and not find unhappiness or boredom.

Something inside that heart said a great many conquests lay ahead and, properly tempted, the whole of the town would sway and in time, falter. The evil one would be pleased and reward the messenger. But this town would offer its own rewards.

The grey haze of temptation swept over the land and lay ankle deep and—for the lack of sight into the supernatural—could be seen by none. Verily, no sign of evil would be foreseen or even felt until the messenger made ready to allow it.

That dark and ominous day didst arrive for any to witness on three days past the celebration of the New

Year. It came in the guise of innocence, announcing its presence from within a girl—a mere teen.

It took over her body as easily as one dons a suit. It bade her make evil where no man would look yet many would dare go—with proper persuasion. As the girl seduced each new man to sin, the messenger grew stronger, it would need that strength to control someone strong willed. Someone like Rose Antonia Riley Ford. Into her, the messenger thought, every man in town would come. And it would have say over all lest it smite them with its power. Power it would soon have. Power it would soon wield.

But not yet.

Winter blew in with a bitter tooth to gnaw at the mortal flesh of the good people of Hemmingforth. Wind, borne of the north, could not be stopped by something as trivial as a wall. And the fires stoked against it did little to bring about true warmth to any souls nearby.

Yet walls were constructed to force its direction in hopes of protecting that mortal flesh. And fires were stoked to head off the burn of the icy north winds. Oft times these very walls were put so deeply upon by that wind they wouldst sway with the rhythm of the music brought about by the gales themselves. And the people huddled together against the threat put to them, pulling ever closer to the fire.

The danger lived and fell upon them as a blanket against the cold whistling outside the flimsy walls. But the truth of its being and purpose was surely lost on the people. For true evil did not reside within the winds. Thus, the people were blinded by their innocence and genuine dependence on a man they called Magistrate.

He, as any other mortal soul, could not save them from the evil, be it the cold, pounding of winter's fist or the messenger sent from the dark lord. The solitude of winter so struck the tiny town even that messenger would not dare come forth and present itself, should it ever have chosen to do so.

Cold is not the way of the evil one. He hath chosen the fires deep in the belly of the Earth for reasons. And, indeed, come spring thaw, many would begrave loved ones taken by the dropping temperatures. This served no purpose nor was it analogous to the messenger's goal.

The young girl's cajoling postponed, and the messenger's strength waning, time slid by as a snail in tree sap and the evil one grew impatient. Hope for an early thaw faded as the cold battered on through February and March. In the end there would be many dead, including some who might succumb to the wiles of a girl who lacked the grace of age to resist.

Any number of weak-spirited men would fall into her web of jasmine and musk, the scents of womanhood she'd not yet achieved. The pools of her eyes would devour them and seduce them. Her body, not yet fully blossomed would become as a receptacle for their seed. All thoughts of decency would be cast aside while in her. And a tiny flame of desire for her would continue to burn within them even after they managed to get away. The evil living among them had taught her well how to use these weapons and others.

Good men of moral standing would seldom take notice of such a girl but the messenger lent her the power to so confuse and entice, few had the fortitude to say, *away!* And many would lay with her as the spring came upon them and the air became warm enough for such fornications to take place outside.

For such as a teen-aged girl would have no home of her own in which to make private her true purpose. So, behind a barn, inside a stable, where the forest became thick, even inside the church as the pastor was about, these became her boudoir. And her tender young body offered release from the lust she, herself placed in their hearts to draw them closer into her. And she collected the seed so craved, though she knew not from whence such cravings sprang.

Her given name, she could hardly remember, Elisabeth...*something*. The strength to retain her true self grew faint with each moment passing even as the thoughts of another became like unto her own. She felt a growing want for the men who entered and knew not how to stop the evil that had overtaken her morality.

At just barely over seventeen, she knew only of chores and mischief. She would shy away from boys because...they were boys. Her and the other girls would giggle and talk about them. Then—homework and chores. But never would they touch one, for truly their immortal souls would be lost. The pastor had said as much in his sermon.

Elisabeth felt her soul slipping away as water from a cup with holes. Even as this, the ninth man, came into her and she felt the pleasure of his warmth, she knew her soul journeyed away and would be kept from her forever. It would languish in the fires of hell as she, all the while, led one man after another away from the cross of his own salvation.

Was such meant to be the whole of her life? Would there be no other place for her to lie but beneath the hardness of a man, all men. Some part of what was left of Elisabeth wept. She made a last noble effort to take back that which had been hers, but she had not the strength and her efforts availed her naught. She slumped beneath this man even as he became mortal inside her, as was the way with each and all of them.

Knowing the deed to be done and be there no turning back, the man left hurriedly, taking his chagrin with him. Elisabeth lay for a moment; still, floating on her thoughts, then gathered her garmenture and slithered into the brightness of an otherwise innocent day.

As she set about the task of imitating a person walking on the street, she saw the face of the man who had so recently been inside her. Without conscience, no reason to evade, she strode ahead with no sign of remorse. The man, to the contrary, studied the small patches of grass that still grew in the street with earnest. His head bobbed from side to side as if in search of retreat.

"Fine day, good sir," Elisabeth spoke, as if naught were out of ordinary.

"F-Fine day, young m-miss," he stammered. Fortune favored him and no one observed his discomfort. He walked on, temporarily extricated, though his desire mounted and he would seek out her immature pleasures again soon, and a smile of devious proportions encroached upon Elisabeth's face.

The hint of a scent brought on by her actions didst not cause her embarrassment but urged her to further debauchery. She studied the path ahead for another tasty treat to explore the stables with. The shadows there appealed to her and cessated her uneasiness.

But empty streets met her eyes and sadness— her heart. She knew despair and solitude before womanhood. In many ways, her young life began similar to Rose's, manipulated by a pull stronger than any control. Elisabeth had as much power to resist as any child.

The beast lay happy within the bosom of the young girl. But its true goal and ultimate fruition would come from occupying the older and ever-more experienced Rose Antonia Riley Ford. She would be the tool with which it would conquer this town and then—the world, perhaps?

The demon lay upon bedrock; resting, plotting, as the girl, Elisabeth, slept. The time had come to exercise the power it had, test its bounds. Its time in the girl—nearly over, it looked upon the heart of Rose once again.

Many a night it visited her bosom, feeling the rise of her chest and the rhythm of her heart. The demon would touch her in that special place; a place no other could touch, or see. A place inside.

She would writhe to the pleasures she thought derived from her own hand and would often wake with embarrassment from such actions. At times she didst pursue such fleeting delights, but always at a time of her choosing and within her control. If she acted out in her sleep, what manner of control did she truly have? Surely even *her* demons had to rest, did they not? Still the creature of darkness had not the strength to dominate such a woman.

A sound! Strong, as though next to its ear, but clearly faraway, drew its attention away. It started. Searching its own feelings to discover those of another, it sought only to know. But truth be told, it feared what it might find, and with good reason. Elisabeth had gone to her father's tool shed. Her intentions…

The demon had to move quickly to interfere. Prevention was imperative; it had to stop her. What she planned…couldn't be allowed. It was not ready.

With an unholy link, established over many months, it could see through her eyes as its own. The rope looked to be three-quarters braid, very durable. The beast moved faster.

The images within its mind altered. It now gazed into the grain of a six-by-six wooden beam—just as the rope slipped over. The images became jumbled, perhaps because it *knew* where they led.

Once inside the shed, the beast stilled. Quiet came to its ears as darkness encroached upon its eyes. When it settled its sight on her body swaying in the air as the reeds of a willow, it stumbled.

With Elisabeth gone, it hadn't yet the power to take Rose; it would have to rely on her *weakness* for aid. The lust within Rose's heart would be that which allowed it access to the deepest regions of her soul. Perhaps it could persuade her with offers of the satisfaction she'd craved even so recently.

The beast had gathered some strength; the rest would be up to Rose.

A warm spring night, Rose wrestled with sheets that did not attack. Sweat beaded on her skin, smooth but toughened from hard work. Her mouth moved but nondescript sounds were all that escaped. Even though her lids stayed closed, it would have been easy for anyone to see her eyes darting from one side to another, up and down, in circles, completely out of control.

In frenzy her hands sought to hide between her legs, although their true purpose became clear within minutes as they found their own way to the tender folds of flesh that lay there—folds that moistened in anticipation of her touch. A reeling mind fought for control but base urges became deviant and proceeded in their own purpose, and at their own pace.

With wild images crashing through her mind and hands frantically jerking to an unheard rhythm, Rose drove herself to spasms that served only one need. Distressed as she slept, the nightmare fed further on by her physical exertions and twisted into something she could not possibly have dreamed up from her own Earthly experiences. She sat up quickly, disoriented, a struggled to breathe.

After realization dawned, she sobbed in despair. She worked at untying the sheets holding her fast and considered that she'd now been forced to become a morning shower person. The sheet knots resisted and she tugged harder, finally falling to the floor in complete disarray. Hysterical laughter dribbled from her lips.

"Can I have no control over these urges? Must I forever succumb to the temptation of the devil? Am I so damned?"

Rose had dreamed before, intense images and feelings, leading to physical interactions. This night had been different. This night something drew her, compelled her, she could feel its lure—its seduction. Something changed and she could decipher none of the images remaining in her early morning mind.

Living alone—perhaps the only good fortune she could tout—she rose without dressing, prepared the morning coffee to brew, and set about the necessity of that shower. She felt a new feeling of warmth inside— warmer than normal. Perhaps she'd fevered during the night. Most times when night fever struck, she bore the mark for many days—usually on the lip. But a healthy body was nothing to be ashamed of, even in a town as prudish as Hemmingforth.

However, no mark appeared and her skin didst feel dry and smooth as always. No sign of fever or other sickness could she find—and so it was that she went about her daily business as if nothing had fallen out of proper place.

Her first official duty was, as always, to the office of the magistrate. On this day, upon entering,

65

she met with silence and dust. Had not the place been occupied as yet this day, and she being late? An eerie foreboding fell over her as she began to look about. She saw no signs to the contrary of order and yet the clouds of bad omens remained.

A singular piece of paper stuck out of the top drawer of Wilford's massive desk. Her curiosity would not allow her to consider looking away as her disobedient hand withdrew the missive. Her heart fluttered and her eyes darted around in search of another presence—any presence—from which she might take leave. Finding none, she moved toward the light and began reading the document.

Be it known that, on this the 28th day of November, in the year of Our Lord, 1807, Wilford Denton Hemmingforth didst willfully and knowingly cheat on an exam, causing disgrace to himself and this institution. His unconscionable act has left a black mark on the school and its faculty that will be difficult to remove.

At the behest of the headmaster, the typical punishment of expulsion has been commuted. While I am not privy to the wisdom behind such a decision, I will abide by it until I can see a way to overturn the decree. The immutable proof of young Mr. Hemmingforth's guilt is on file. I saw myself as his hand swayed toward another student and his eye turned to examine the other's answers.

*Conduct of this caliber is unacceptable.
An honorable school such as this must not be
allowed to tarnish itself by overlooking such
actions even for the most exemplary reasons.
To my knowledge this is the first time this
facility has been witness to such an abomination
of the Code of Conduct, written so long ago by
those great scholars that founded the school.*

*I have more than enough proof to take
this higher, to the Magistrate himself, if need be.
But I write this more as a dedication. If by
chance, I am not conciliated in this venture, I
shall immediately and forthwith tender
my resignation with as much haste as I can
muster.*

*For I will not remain bedfellow to a
criminal mind—not he who would commit the
crime, nor he who wouldst cover it up.*

I do declare on this day, my intention.

*Marcus Danforth Brody
Professor of Practical Law
Walton University*

When she'd finished, her teared eyes glanced toward the door—still undisturbed by the passage of even one soul, save her own. The parchment would not return to its original hiding place willingly and Rose pulled at the drawer. It came freely. Inside were any number of papers, all of which appeared as official and ominous as the first. She dared not read further—not only for fear of exposure, but of what she might learn.

Wilford had cheated. This alone brought a chill to Rose's heart. The stalwart man, God-fearing, upstanding, community leader, and Magistrate, possessed dark clouds in his past. Although Rose preferred not to judge another lest she be judged for her own less-than-proper life, she could not help but conclude that those who have a dark cloud often have several—perhaps many.

If she could be with such a man, she would know the truth—all truths. These truths, to which she had right, could only show her the man inside, bringing her deeper love through understanding. She would view his darkest secrets and then forgive him. Then a thought ran through her mind.

Would she be willing to give up all her darker secrets for his judgment? If so, would he be so quick to forgive? Rose shuddered to think of the calamity that would ensue should Wilford ever find the truth about her own past. She vowed that he would never be privy to such knowledge as long as she drew breath.

Without warning a tingle slithered through her body. This kind of tingle she knew from experience. Her promiscuous days gave her knowledge average, proper women would never know. The desires, dark and strong, welled up and tugged at the very core of her womanhood. While this was common on many days before, those times were passed and Rose had managed control over them for quite some time. That they should suddenly reappear surprised her more than if someone had walked in and caught her rifling through Wilford's desk.

The few memories that came to mind as she reminded of her past should not have been sufficient to bring about such strong urges. And yet, here she stood, in the magistrate's office, inappropriately going through private mailings, and being overwhelmed by deviant needs. Could the knowledge of Wilford's unclean past have provoked her own in such a manner?

She thought not. However, the urge to drop her hands and rub the desire away became too much. Knowing she would read them later, Rose returned the letters to the desk drawer and made her way to the shadows of the office behind her own desk. Once there, out of sight of anyone that might enter, but where she could clearly see the door, she began a ritual she'd not partaken of in several weeks.

Dousing the fires that burned within took an act scorned by God, but the alternative would be even less accepted. She'd thought herself well past being under the influence of such feelings and counted herself far better off for it—knowing her return to salvation would include abstention from such thoughts. *Where is the strong voice of Wilford when I need him so?*

Once finished she found herself still so overcome with need that she began again almost instantly. A second brief peak took her and she felt little better. Once the third came and went she began to concern for her health—hardly noticing if anyone had entered the office. She knew something was very wrong, as she could not withdraw her hands without feeling nauseous for a moment, then her hands would fall quickly back to her lap.

Slumped back in her creaking wooden chair, she pushed for another pleasure moment and then another, hoping each would bring the great release that would allow her to remove the devilish hands and focus on things proper. Several moments felt quite intense and yet her need continued. *Is there no satisfying this need? Can I not withdraw my hands from their fiendish work and set them to rights again?*

Rose struggled to make her hands obey her will. They'd gone about their own business far long enough and she would begin the work of her station. To do this, she needed her hands to be free of their self-chosen obligation. Time and again she raised them, thinking this time she could free herself from this devil's grip, then they would plummet back to their dark work that felt so good at first but now became quite painful. She knew not what drew them back—only that the urge was not of her own design.

The fight ensued. In her favor, Rose fought valiantly to bring about an end to the debacle. Try as she might she could not gain control over her wanton hands—if indeed she ever had such power. Losing count and most all coherence, she started upright at the sound of the front door being swung back with fury and banging against the storage cabinets that stood two-high behind it.

A burly man with dirty clothes entered, sporting an unkempt beard and scraggly hair. He paused to look around as his eyes adjusted to the shadow's contrast from the bright sun that filled the street outside. His recovery seemed to come quickly by Rose's measure. After hardly a moment he noticed her and approached. Two other men came in and stood behind the first. She managed to sit upright and appear proper, although one hand remained beneath the desk, continuing on its evil mission even as he spoke to her.

"There a man here named Hemmingforth?" His poor English and uneducated manner came through in loud tones and terrible breath.

"I-I..." Rose stammered beneath the man's stern voice and the unrelenting stroke of her fingers. "No," she managed.

"Damn, missed him again." The man looked around, then snapped back to Rose. "What is that peculiar smell?"

"Smell? I smell nothing, good sir."

The man offered a grunt in response. "When did you see him last?"

"Yesterday," she squeaked.

"So he's still in town?"

Rose chirped a bit but made no comprehendible noise. Obviously the man understood the noise to mean 'yes'. He stepped back. Perhaps he realized that he frightened the young girl.

71

"I'll be back."

As quickly as he'd entered, the door closed behind him and the other two with a loud slam, shaking dust from the rafters. He may have been overzealous but Rose considered it might be more. She thought perhaps he could be angry at Wilford. She feared he might intend harm and considered how to warn the man she loved. But she knew not whence he'd gone or how to find him.

At the very least, her worry, in the end, had distracted her wayward hands.

The man slithered in from behind, causing little noise but making his presence known. The evil snake—Rose knew it to be the same from the Garden of Eden—entered her with the gentleness of a man intent on causing pain. Delirious, she fought to recognize the surroundings, and perhaps the man that violated her in such a manner.

Although Sodom had been destroyed and she knew her act warranted damnation, yet she thrust herself back against his lustful advances in desire. Unable to resist the call of the flesh, she not only participated, but—*God save me*—enjoyed. The pressure asserted inside her caused pain and still she called for it to continue with every ounce of her being. She could not have asked for more if she begged out loud, which she dared not do for fear of being caught in such an act.

Again she made effort to turn and know the man who certainly knew her. With her dress thrown up her back and her petticoat around her ankles, she felt much more exposed than just her body. Somehow her soul lay out for all to see—the urges that grew within her had now come out for sunshine and she stood vulnerable.

Wicked thoughts ran through her head. She drew images of each and every man in town taking turns in her as she leaned against the fence and waited—exposed and offering. More than simple images, she *wanted* them in her, fighting for a turn, coming around for seconds, following her home, unable to resist.

Bile rose in her throat juxtaposing the joy she felt in her nether region. As the man finished and left traces of himself behind, she turned to catch a last chance look at his face, to know, at least, who she'd lain with. If she were to risk the budding love she had with Wilford, let it not be for some passing moment with a man she hardly knew.

Though turning away, his face offered enough for her to see. One of the two men who had visited the Magistrate's office on that very morn, now shuffled away carrying with him a confused look. She could see his despair. He knew not why he'd come. Rose could find no memory of the experience, either—save the ending. Had she lured him? Did he force her? Would anyone in town have noticed?

But in Rose's deepest consciousness remained one paramount question, rising above all others, drawing her focus from all others. She focused on it, turning it over in her mind to see it from all sides. The question shown clear, but the answer eluded her as much as any other she'd encountered in her life.

Why have I taken up my old ways once again?

The demon lay in the soft folds at the bottom of Rose's heart, warm and cozy. It found tugging the right strings easy with a woman half way to hell already. She took the journey with so little provocation; the demon hardly had to work at all. Life would only get easier from this point forward and the town was as good as handed over to the evil one.

Looking out through the eyes of the woman, it desired a further test of her obedience and devotion—if not to him, at least to the desires that burned between her legs, desires of the past never fully quenched. It watched as she walked through town trying to avoid others, hoping to take back control.

"Nay, control is mine," it scratched at her, even though she could not truly hear.

But the demon knew it'd won the battle, even though it did not understand her unorthodox method of coupling. It could see inside her heart and knew her desires had been rekindled and, with a little of its help, would burn hotter than the fires of hell itself.

The seed had been planted. It would grow.

Rose walked awkwardly as the pain kept her from proper gait. She struggled to portray a lady-like image while intentionally avoiding populated areas for fear of having to address questions for which she had no answers. She wanted only to go home. Once there she would pray for forgiveness and strength to overcome the urges welling within.

As she turned north toward the part of town where her small ranch stood, she spotted Jimmy Waller. A man in his own right, but just barely, he looked somehow more enticing than Rose could ever remember. Her mouth became dry as she turned her step slightly in his direction. Life became fuzzy.

When her mind cleared enough for coherent thought, she discovered herself lying on her back in the hay with Jimmy on top, pounding into her like a rabbit. His youth drew him to finish in a very short time. His seed shooting into her, she wondered why she didn't feel disappointment as she would have in the past.

As soon as the deed was done and she found herself back on her way home, Rose pondered. Something had surely changed in her. In the past, her urges were for her own satisfaction and yet she enjoyed pain from one man, and brevity from another. Neither of which would satisfy the needs of a woman like her.

Nevertheless, she felt satisfied. Nay, euphoric, complete, as if her day could not have concluded without her dangerous liaison along the way. Never had feelings such as these entered her mind. Had the devil completely taken over her soul and she no longer walked the path of salvation she'd sought so long?

Once inside the privacy of her own home, she knelt at her bedside, sobbing, calling upon the name of the Lord to come into her life and bring His salvation. *Wield Your mighty sword, just and true, and cut away the evilness that dwells within my very body. Bring me the strength to stand against the call of animal lust overflowing in my soul. Wash away the blackness that hast befallen me, Oh Lord, that I may, once again follow in Your footsteps. Lead me…away…*

The words became difficult as she felt pain inside.

…from…the evil…that would…dwell…inside…

Rose took deep breaths, forcing each word out, focusing on her lips to form each syllable properly. She would not allow her grammar to slip while she spoke to God.

...the...body...of...a...girl...who...would...be...y our...

Rose collapsed to the floor. Unconscious before her head hit the wood, she fell instantly to a dream state that had her tossing about like someone demon possessed. Her dark dream images flashed into her mind with increasing speed.

When she woke in the middle of the night she felt surprise at how many of the images remained. At first she could see the parade of men, lined up, trousers down, taking turns in her as she held tightly to the fence—the only thing around solid enough to offer support. For hours she collected each seed and waited for the next, only having to wait for the briefest of seconds. Then another man would enter her. Some even sodomized her.

Afterward, she saw images of women, gripping her breasts, twisting her nipples, as another man gave up his mortality inside her from behind. The women watched in glee as each took his turn. Sometimes they too were without clothes, most only from waist up but many completely—even old Mrs Whippel, whom Rose regretted seeing naked more than anything else. Rose felt like she'd been shackled in the square and each of the townspeople could walk by and throw vegetables at her or whip her at whim.

But she wore not shackles. Her hands remained free to move. Yet move she did not. She waited, longing for the next and the next, moaning under the pinching pressure of the women who also took turns at her chest. Pain and pleasure mixed together so well, like an onion soup with just the right amount of beef flavor. She yearned for each and every diabolical moment as she sank further into depravity.

And the images became darker, more exotic and deviant.

In the dream she closed her eyes. Not in embarrassment, but waiting—yearning for the next entry which took longer. In her delirium she felt a tap on her head. When she opened her mouth to speak she discovered a man there, as well. A thing to do she'd never imagined and could barely tolerate—and still she wanted it.

In time, perhaps minutes, three men entered her at once. Although she could not, heretofore, have imagined how it would be possible, it nevertheless happened. She could not fathom how all could fit, but she wanted it. She wanted it desperately. If she'd known she could have asked for such a thing she would have begged. She thought she had sunk to the deepest depths possible. But darkness had not fully fallen on her dream state as yet.

She felt the stinging sensation across her buttocks—sending shivers of delight up her spine. Rose had felt pain before, even from childhood when she'd earned a stern beating from her father. But nothing had given her body such a surge of joy as this had. Perhaps, she thought as she dreamed, it is because the men are using me and it feels so good.

She turned at the second strike of pain and noticed a man behind her—inside her—using a switch across her bare skin. In her dream the man's face became her father's. But her father had never touched her inappropriately like this man was doing. The pain and pleasure mixed to send her somewhere past delirium and into the twilight world where shadows came to life and your head could spin and you lose your way in a moment.

She felt another stripped tree branch slap across her back and still another striking her underneath—striping her belly and breasts with red welts of pain. The pain continued, as did the penetrations. Her mouth filled with one man after another, she could hardly scream for the torture to stop. And she wasn't sure she wanted it to stop. A deep seated, nymphomaniacal force drove her to willingly accept and even crave the continued degradation.

At some point, long after she'd lost track of time and count, everything stopped. Two women stayed near her head, on either side. They focused on something of interest Rose could not quite see. Something to do with her hands on the fence. *Oh, they're tying my hands to the rail. That's nice.*

Her delirious mind swung through each image as if it simply watched a play and someone else occupied the stage. Rose couldn't have resisted even if

79

she wanted to. And she definitely did not want to. If she could have spoken, she would have asked for more.

Her mouth, suddenly devoid of manhood, now filled again with a ball and a cloth tied around her head holding it in. So her hands were tied and her mouth was tied. She looked to her feet. Sure enough, two men drove tent stakes into the ground next to her feet and two more women were tightly knotting rope around them and to her ankles. Rose felt powerless against the onslaught of what she felt sure was coming. A part of her feared, but another longed.

The woman on her right caught a string tossed from behind where Rose could see. She pulled it closer. The woman on Rose's left had one just like it. They walked their strings forward to where Rose's hands were tethered to the fence. They held tightly against something that jerked and tugged.

Confused, Rose tried to turn her head but was held fast by something or someone she could not see. But she knew something was back there, closing in, breathing on her in forceful snorts. She heard the bray of a horse at the same time she felt the splitting pain between her legs. She screamed against the ball in her mouth but very little sound came out. Pulling against the ties cut her skin and tiny droplets of blood dripped to the grass beneath.

She tried desperately to emancipate herself and soothe the pain wrought by some unseen demon man. After a moment she began to relax. The feeling became quite tolerable almost a pleasure. Her needs began to rise once again and she could feel release approaching. When she felt large amounts of something washing inside her, she went over the edge, succumbing to the ecstasy of peaking in such pain.

Her body collapsed, falling off the skewer that held her moments before. Exhausted, she simply fell to the ground and lay in a bath of sweat and other fluids. Her mind, sated and unable to focus, forced her eyes to glance up. The stallion stood proud: unaware of his indecent exposure. His large genital swung, dripping, glistening with juices from Rose.

She could not believe. The vomit she felt earlier rose and did not stop. Tears streamed from her eyes. No sobs could be heard even as her bonds were released and the ball fell from her mouth. Finally free she pulled herself into a fetal position at the base of the fence and once again looked at the stallion. It was no longer a stallion, but a demon. It stood as a man, although bent and twisted with evil. It had not skin.

The demon's penis, larger than any she'd ever seen, larger even than the stallion's, began to rise and enlarge. As it came to full glory, reaching near to the demon's neck and chin, Rose shuddered knowing that, as the demon was a horse, it entered her as a horse. This, much larger instrument, would surely rend her womanly parts perhaps completely in two.

The demon began to laugh a sharp, raspy sound that hurt Rose's ears and its penis bounced with the laughter. She looked around and saw everyone standing near her. They all laughed with the demon.

81

Most remained unclothed as though modesty had been abandoned for sake of the demon's will. She forced her sore hand to make the sign of the cross and the laughter grew.

Then the demon drew near and the laughter abated. Rose could already see the moisture dripping from its excited manhood. The men and women each grabbed her limbs, pulling her apart, spread, ready, inviting the demon inside. Her pudendum called for the penetration, but her mind didst tremble. The evil thing mounted her, poised for maximum insertion. Rose held her breath as the demon lifted its hips, like cocking a musket. Terror, beyond insanity, rent her unconscious in her dream, even as she awakened in reality.

Now sitting at her table she shivered in abject fear. Though only a dream, its vividness stabbed at her soul with all the pain of a real experience. And she could not shake the feeling that more than just dreams happened this night. Of course that would be absurd. She knew no one would treat her so and no demons existed in Hemmingforth.

Then she noticed her wrists were sore and on her right one—a small laceration.

When next she saw Wilford she ran to him for protection against something she neither could see nor explain. She'd done nothing. *Haven't you?* But even telling such a story could prove destructive. Dimorphic demons that seduced her and made the whole town partake? Even as she said it within the safety of her own mind it sounded preposterous. And completely unbelievable. When he asked her what's wrong, she could not possibly say. Only that she needed him.

"Where hast thou travelled, Mr. Hemmingforth?"

"Across the plains to the east. I had to conduct a matter of urgent business there. News came of a child possessed by a demon."

"Is that not a task best left to clergy?"

"Sometimes it takes more than one man to move a mountain, Miss Ford."

"Forgive me, sir. I meant no disrespect. But a man has come to town. He seeks you. He calls you by name."

"And did he offer his?"

"He did not." Somehow, Rose felt embarrassed by her ineptitude. In all truth, the burly man would probably not have given his name even if asked.

"Perhaps he will come by again today," Wilford said.

"He will, sir. He seemed most persistent."

"Did he, now? Did this urgency, by chance, have anything to do with another demon possession?"

83

"Not to my knowledge, but he spoke not of his mission. Only that he would engage with you. I think very little will deter him."

Wilford smiled. "You have done well, Miss Ford. Return to your duties. I shall be along in due time."

"As you wish, Mr. Hemmingforth." She couldn't be sure how to accept his compliment. But returning to work brought her some ease of mind as she now had focus. That is, until she passed through the doorway and spied her own chair; the memories of her uncontrollable hands came flooding back with fervor.

Apprehension flooded her body as she approached her position, knowing the evil must surely reside there, perhaps under the chair. Of course her Sunday school teachings told her that evil could live anywhere and only needed a catalyst. *Is that what I've become? A catalyst for evil? And what of the day Wilford discovers?*

Rose pushed such thoughts from her head as she set about her daily duties. This time, apparently, she had no reason to fear, though that strong emotion had overwhelmed her only moments before. But this time her hands did as she bade and no desires came to call.

Shadows grew long and her eyes tired when she next looked up from her work. Duty had kept Wilford away the rest of the day. She would have to close the office by herself. Although she closed many times and could accomplish the feat without needing to double check, eeriness befell her. She half expected some dark urge to pull at her hands or carry her feet to the barnyard. Perhaps the gruff stranger would reappear, frightening her more than before.

But once again her fears were in vain. No one called on the Magistrate's office and her hands minded their master. *Which master is that?* She meandered home, hoping Wilford would be seated at his desk on the morrow.

"Ah, Miss Ford. A pleasant morning to you."

"And to you, sir." She half expected him to not be there and yet she longed for his presence with every nerve in her body.

"A report came in this morning, to the sheriff's office."

"Oh, nothing too terrible, I hope."

"Three men were found dead just south of town."

"Dear God! How dreadful. Anyone we know?"

"I don't think so. Strangers, according to Sheriff Cornell."

"And the sheriff saw fit to inform you of such unpleasant news?"

"Being the Magistrate, I am privy to such dealings. He often consults me in legal issues. I am, after all, trained in these matters."

"Ah yes. That you are," Rose finished, turning toward her desk.

"Is there something wrong, Miss Ford?"

"Oh, no. Not at all, sir. I just wondered who those three men might be."

"And did anything come to mind?"

"I thought of the men who sought you and thought perhaps it might be them."

"Yes." Wilford seemed to accept her suggestion and mulled it deeply. "Perhaps they came for me and I was not here. Then, as they waited for the next day when they could return and address their business, some tragedy overtook them."

Rose found her desk and sat safely behind it as Wilford began to pace, speaking to himself maniacally. She'd never seen him like this before. Though much was mumbling, she could understand snippets—not quite every other word.

"If they…why didn't…could I be…how can I help?"

And so he rambled on, incoherent and disjointed, Rose allowed him room to explore whatever turmoil rampaged through his mind. When his eyes cleared and he spoke to Rose again, his mind seemed as focused as ever. But what he said took her aback more than her dream the night before.

"Miss Ford."

"Yes, Mr. Hemmingforth?"

"I thought perhaps…that is, the annual town picnic is coming soon and I thought—if no one has already asked—you might agree to accompany me."

"Mr. Hemmingforth! We've known each other little more than six months. It is a bit too soon to be courting, is it not?"

"I have been in town for nearly two years. Who is to decide at what time we first met."

"Is that not deceitful?"

"Perhaps you are right. Forgive me, Miss Ford. I overstepped my proper place."

Rose discovered victory wasn't so sweet after all. "I think I would like to go to the picnic with you, Mr. Hemmingforth."

His demeanor brightened visibly. He stood taller and his smile radiated his joy. She could not help but return it. "Do you not care about the proper way for us to conduct ourselves in public, then?"

Rose stood and approached him. She made one last glance around the room for assurance, despite knowing they were alone.

"I think an observant man like yourself already knows I have feelings for you—I have had since I first laid eyes on you. I care little for the whisperings of the townspeople. I've never been concerned with such drivel."

"So I have heard."

Rose became suspicious, stiffening. "What have you heard?"

"Nothing that would prevent me from asking you to the picnic."

She smiled. A true gentleman to the last. How could she do anything but accept?

The impromptu band, made mostly of homemade instruments, could not have sounded much more dissonant. Local farmers, she knew all their names, sat at one end of the field and did their best. Rose, who'd experienced the finer compositions of great masters like Mozart and Dvorák, knew the difference. To the contrary, many of the people living in Hemmingforth could not tell, or chose not to care. They danced spritely and laughed loudly.

Rose thought they could adapt the same attitude toward her and Wilford. It may not sit well on their palate, but they could just keep their cares to themselves. She had wanted to be with Wilford since the beginning and she wouldn't allow a budding relationship to turn sour on the count of the inability of other people to keep their condescending mouths shut. She needed no acceptance from them. She never had in the past.

A brief shudder ran through her as she thought about what stories Wilford might have been told. Her only comfort came from the fact he still asked her and he walked proudly next to her as they entered the town square in full view of everyone else. Rose caught a few unfriendly stares but Wilford seemed not to notice.

Rose knew he did not have a blind eye and therefore probably saw all, but rather chose to ignore such condescencions in favor of the more Christian attitude of forgiveness. Something that resembled real love bloomed in her heart and she looked up at the eyes of the man standing next to her. He caught glimpse of her stare.

"Are you uncomfortable? Would you like to leave?"

"I feel wonderful. I do not wish to leave, but if we must, let us be together."

"A few upturned noses do not bother me. From that angle, I see directly up their nostrils at how tiny their brains are."

Rose could not suppress her laughter. She reached over to grip his arm which elicited more glares. To Rose, it could become a game. The more brazen she became, the more open their mouths would fall. She imagined their jaws would reach the limit before her daring. An image she could not squelch flashed into her mind.

She saw herself against the horse post, bent over as in her dream, dress thrown up her back. Wilton took advantage without shame. She could imagine people running, covering the eyes of their children, even some who stayed and watched—feigning disgust and horror while delighting in the immoral show.

She pushed the image out of her mind with some effort. She felt no sense indulging in such fantasies; they would only lead to troubles she could not undo. If she began to feel those urges and could not control her hands, the square offered no privacy of which she could partake and no excuse for an early exit came to mind. In all, it would look far too suspicious and she would have no answers to the inevitable questions everyone would throw later.

All this and how bad it would make Wilford look. Perhaps some would think he had mistreated or insulted her. And worst is how he would feel. She thought he would be diminished and embarrassed, even though he'd done nothing inappropriate. She could not allow it. She pushed the effort harder, burying the erotic images floating around her mind.

As a distraction, Rose asked Wilford if he could dance. His twisted face suggested he would refuse, but he must have recanted the thought at seeing her joy. She grabbed his hand as casually as possible and skipped to the tiny area where everyone else who dared, danced. Her happiness culminated in her grace and well executed dance moves. Wilford, quite to her surprise, matched her technique precisely. They looked like a well-practiced stage act.

While many sat in awe, there still remained an undertone of judgment in the faces of people Rose had known most of her life. Some of them called themselves friend. She'd been to many of their homes, brought food, helped with the young when their mother was sick, and acted like a proper neighbor. However, now they didst not act so.

"It would seem, when I'm needed, I'm accepted. Otherwise, I am to be ostracized. For what, I do not know."

"Worry not, fair maiden, for I shall bear you succor and you shall not want for love."

She looked at Wilford as if he'd spoken in jest. But his face betrayed none. Try as she might, she could not fathom the depth of his mind nor the truth of his spirit. Once again she remembered the writing from his desk. He'd been cast out, a common criminal. And then men came looking, seeking his presence with urgency. And those men were now dead. Could Wilford have had something to do with that? Could he kill?

She looked into his eyes once again and saw no anger, no malice, no evil. She sought the comfort he offered, leaning just a bit closer, feeling the warmth of his body, though the summer solstice had just passed. His heat cast out the chill she felt from the eyes of others.

She'd not mentioned leaving and yet she did feel a need to be away from prying gazes. But she thought remaining would be more appropriate for her station—and, indeed, if she and Wilford would begin courting, there would be many such opportunities for people to judge or judge not. They would simply have to get over it.

"I could not be more grateful for your words of promise. I sought no reward, only to be accepted as equal. If this is not to be, among these people—my neighbors and friends, then I shall live without it. Jesus was persecuted as well. I am no better than He. The time has come for me to be with you and they shall see the happiness you bring me. Understanding, if it not be given now, will have to come later. I promise you, only *their* sleep will be disturbed, not mine."

Wilford laughed. "Child, you say the most uncanny things. I do believe Mrs. Cowen has made some punch. I've overheard several people exclaiming how marvelous it tastes. Would you care for some refreshment?"

"Oh, do fetch us some, good sir," she mocked, batting her eyelashes. "I would rather enjoy a cool drink."

Wilford went. He returned quickly with two tall cups of pink liquid and handed one to Rose, smiling handsomely. Chivalrous and mannered, he bowed slightly as she took the cup and brought it to her lips.

Oddly, Rose thought the elixir quite bland, offering only the savor of sweetness perhaps from honey. But the sun shone high and after drinking she did feel refreshed. She concluded that all she'd needed might have been some sugar. In the end, with an empty glass, she just felt much better about the day in all.

"Quite good," she lied as she handed the beaker back to Wilford. He took it and his own empty and returned them to the table from whence he first took them. Mrs. Cowen nodded her head to him in thanks. Rose assumed he'd paid her a compliment on the pallid liquid. If she'd returned the cups herself, she might not have been so gracious. The liquid was drank, the cups emptied, that should be sign enough of the delight it offered. Beyond that, compliments became lies.

When Wilford returned to the seat he'd left Rose on, and finding it empty, his eyes searched the horizon but discovered no sign of her. Confused he began walking about, but not asking anyone for sure they would scoff and tell him he'd be better off without her. He felt no such relief and continued his search in silence.

But no one even bothered to ask if they could help. No one noticed that he searched, or they did but chose to look away. *Would they turn their backs on me so quickly, and because of my association with Rose? Could they be so small-minded? They do not deserve one such as she.* Frustrated with their apathy, he strode on through the small crowd searching, sniffing for her perfume, looking for any—even the slightest—sign of his Rose.

Once away from the main group, all chattering about daily events which everyone already knew, he managed to hear other sounds. Sounds that came from different directions. Animals brayed about, creating their own special music, perhaps speaking to one another. But one noise Wilford could not so easily identify. He sought it out.

Behind a barn, as the afternoon sun set heavy, he saw the sight of his life. He watched in abject horror as the vision unfolded its devious tale, shaking him to his roots. His mouth fell open but no sound would come, though he knew not what to say at such a sight.

Wilford watched as a man—pants around his knees—pounded into some willing beauty beneath him, lying in tall grass. Her legs raised high and her voice a low growl, she drew the man into her, calling for each thrust, begging for no end to come. Female legs curled and her feet pushed at his back, forcing him deeper. Her wanton willingness accosted Wilford's soul more so than seeing such an act out in the open.

The man's eyes crossed and lips twisted as he squirmed his last into the maiden. Then he rose and adjusted himself. When the man turned to return to the picnic, Wilford saw his face clearly. Though he knew not the man's name, the look shone through clear. He was bewildered and contrite. He continued adjusting until he appeared normal and made his way back without seeing Wilford.

Then the woman rose. Her guttural chantings disturbed Wilford in a way he could not understand. She stood, fully nude, and bent for her clothing. When she again became upright, Wilford could see her face—the face of his beloved. Rose.

A sharp pain struck his chest and he fell to his knees. The image of beauty he saw in her body did little to alleviate the despair in his heart. He looked again, through the rungs of the fence and watched. She'd managed to get on her petticoat and worked mindlessly to finish—but not in any hurry Wilford could detect.

Her undergarment buttoned in the front, leaving small openings all the way down. She stopped a moment and examined the lowest of these, fingering her nether region. She withdrew the finger and brought it to her nose, breathing deeply the aroma that he felt certain remained there. He turned quickly, not wanting to see what he thought she would do next with that same finger.

When he looked back, she stood in the same place and in the same state of dress. But she looked directly at him, even though he could not be seen by mortal eye. But her eyes didst not spring from mortality. She glared in a way that spoke evil. Her eyes drew Wilford's energy right from his very body. He felt sure Rose's eyes glowed, with a red hue. Fear took over—far stronger than disgust, cutting deeper than betrayal. He took to his feet and made way back to his sanctorum.

Although the Magistrate Office was not the place of his dwelling, he spent much more time there than any other place. He felt safety amongst the furnishings and flotsam of a different life. All his focus, his idealism, his hold on reality came crashing down about his head and shoulders. He physically ducked, even though nothing substantial came close to hurting him.

But the desk supported him, protected him, comforted him. He gripped its edges and worked to control his breathing. He'd heard the stories loose lips cared to impart, but believed little. No one said anything about her eyes. This incident might not be borne of the same rumors spoken before, if such rumors could at all be trusted.

Something evil had taken hold of his beloved Rose. She would not have looked at him—or anyone else, for that matter—in such a way. And the act, how could she sink to such depths so casually and in open view of the public? Had she not decency? What if someone had seen? Perhaps even a child might have innocently wandered around that barn, and she cared not?

As he thought through the pain, he realized the act might be forgivable. The red eyes and demonic growling were unholy and truly evil. Those things, whatever caused her to do them, would have to be exorcised. She needed his help and he determined not to disappoint her. He sat up straighter, knowing his path, his duty—his only hope. For true love dwelled on the other side of those eyes—the unpossessed eyes, the blue eyes.

He longed to see her smile, once again innocent and fresh, looking at him with what he could only interpret as budding love. He could not repay all the wrongs he'd done, but somehow God blessed him with such honest love. Rose needed his help and he would give his very life if need be. Surely with a past as unclean as Wilford's, God would ask for penance. He would accept that penance, embrace it, satisfy it. He must find a way to keep her close. He knew a way. Perhaps the only way.

Wilford, lost in his own deep thoughts, jumped as the door swung open and late day gloom washed in, bringing dust with it. He looked up and saw the raw face of Rose, searching, fearful. When she spotted him, she relaxed and smiled, slouching slightly—a motion Wilford told her on several occasions he thought very uncomely.

"Wilford. I mean, Mr. Hemmingforth. There you are. When I lost you at the picnic I thought you'd abandoned me because of what the others were saying. I could not find you. I searched. Why did you not return to where I waited?"

"Why?" Wilford hesitated. Her eyes betrayed no untruth. She spoke as she felt. Somehow she knew not what she had done. He did not pretend to understand, only to care. And he needed no pretense for that. Stepping down from his desk platform, he approached her. "While it does not displease me to

97

hear my name upon your lips, it would be inappropriate for you to utter such a thing in front of others. At least wait until we can be wed."

"W-Wed?" Rose stepped back.

"Darling," Wilford continued, unsure what spurred him on and what end he sought. "Is it not what you want, as well?"

"I've thought of little else since I first saw you arrive in town."

"Then why can we not speak of it? We are alone."

"I-I just, how could I have been prepared?"

"You feel even as I," he said.

But she gathered not his true meaning. "I would try and make you a wonderful wife, Wilford. But I must speak with you about a matter of utmost urgency."

"You are troubled. Come and sit. Tell me what troubles you, my dear."

"I have such visions, I see things I could hardly describe."

"Dreams, you mean. Tell me of your dreams."

"I think they are more than mere dreams. I do not know, but something frightens me about them."

"Sit," he bade her.

When he sat next to her, he noticed something that shook him deeply. He could smell the intimacy on her. The act from barely ten minutes ago, still lingered on her as perfume. Though completely distracting, he struggled to focus on the matter at hand. A demon had possessed his beloved. In her normal state, she professed her love for him. When taken from him, she sought comfort in other ways—ways he could not accept or ignore.

"Can you describe these visions?"

"You do not believe. I can see in your eyes. Wilford, how can you say you love me and not believe?"

"Darling, didst thou not say these were visions? I believe you see, but I do not fear they will harm you. If I seem cavalier, do not take offense. I am here. I will help you. I promise. Now tell me of your visions."

"First you must promise to remember these are only visions. I would not become unlike the women you see about town. I've had a past, Wilford. I past of which I am not proud. But what I see is not the same. It is evil. I can feel it. I fear it dwells within me and I know not how to remove it."

"I promise I will not have you ostracized for simply telling me stories. For the sake of my title of Magistrate, what you tell me shall remain nothing more. Therefore, no action will be necessary—whether legal or moral. For they are only stories."

Rose smiled. "I believe you."

"So, your visions? How many have you had?"

"Many. I've lost count. They come day or night. I have no control and when they pass I find myself disoriented and frightened. However, I clearly remember details about them. They are of me— partaking of unspeakable acts. Lewd and lascivious behavior unbecoming of a lady. In fact, I dare say they would be considered unbecoming of a lowly dog. And yet I am there, each and every time, participating, enjoying, longing for more. It's more than just recurring; I believe I am calling it back."

"The vision?"

"Indeed."

"One cannot call upon a dream. Don't you see how foolish this all is? Surely you don't believe you leave your home or place of employment and perform intimate liaisons with strange gentlemen? Even saying it sounds absurd."

Rose sat back, unprepared she was for his revelation. How could he have known of the details of her visions? Did he know more? And how much could he see? How much would he understand and forgive? But if she didst only dream them, was forgiveness necessary? So many questions for which she had no answers.

"How did you know?"

"Know what?"

"What my dreams were about?"

Now it was Wilford's turn to sit back. In his mandatory French classes he'd learned a term they use. *Faux pas.* Had he committed such a bumbling act? He searched his memory, examining his words...and hers. She had not mentioned the truth about her dreams. He'd said it himself. *Perhaps it is time for all truths to come out.*

Rose contemplated the juxtaposition of her lusty calls brought forth from within and those from some, as yet unknown source without. Although her life before may have been spiraling toward an eternity of hellfire, she believed it to be hers to squander. Now she felt as another woman. Fear mingled with the scents of a life of promiscuity.

Someone or something else pulled against her resolve and she drew ever closer to the fiery afterlife. According to the word of God, works alone do not a path to Heaven make. But by works, and truly with no intervention—divine or otherwise—may we enter the gates of eternal damnation

Every ounce of her fortitude backed up and stood for morals even as her hand lowered toward the object of her lust. He waited, exposed, stiff, frightened. The man's eyes twitched in all directions, settling on nothing, even as his anticipation brought him to the brink of ecstasy.

Her hand made intimate contact and his breath caught sharp in his chest. The tension building to the moment or the sultry beauty deep in her eyes, or perhaps both, cursed him with a quick response, quicker than normal. He was over before Rose could mount the steed projecting from his hips.

She looked at the mess in her hand and the muscle relaxing beside it. She felt as though something valuable had been stolen from her. Anger coursed through her and she looked into the sheepish face of the man, satisfied by a mere touch. Fire spewed forth from her eyes, the fire of true hell, and the flesh peeled from the bones of the man almost as sudden as the moment of satisfaction he'd stolen from her.

A kind of horror slapped at Rose's mind as she gazed speechlessly upon the result of her temper. She knew not from whence the fire had come and she froze to the spot, watching the steam of her breath dancing in the brisk air and mingling with the smolder from the body.

Truly there was a power within her. A power of evil, great it was. But she controlled it, not. It indeed stood in power over her and she—its helpless, willing subject. Rose knew not how to rid herself of whatever possession had befallen her. And at stake, nothing less than her immortal soul.

She waited as if for someone to apprehend her and yet none came. Confused, she found a lone thought floating inside. She grasped at it and recoiled. A passage she knew well, but the antithesis of appropriate for what had just happened, what *she* had just done.

Moses quoth: *"...and God looked upon what he had done. And it was good."*

Rose felt as if bile would surely rise up from her feet, through her entire body and out her mouth. Running seemed the only answer. She willed her feet to make haste. They began their way to the safety of her own home.

Once there, Rose laid in bed, fighting back the tears—her only companion. An evil *had* taken her over. She did not envision her unholy liaisons, she *lived* them. She really did those terrible things. And Wilford had seen. Worst of all things, he had witnessed her deviant, casual, sexual depravity. More tears came, flowing freely, soaking her pillow.

She prayed—what to do, what to do. If God could not show her a solution, from where would she find such a thing? No one—no man could fight a demon. Oh, the pastor spoke of fire and brimstone, but he stood short of stature and wide of belly. Were he to face a true demon he would likely defecate himself. And the red of his nose suggested he spoke more to a bottle of whiskey than to God.

She could not live as she did. A tragedy approached. She could see Wilford quickly being forced to stand for righteousness and forsaking her to the judgment of the town tribunal. They would, of course, be forced to burn her at the stake in the name of the one true God, though he would infer forgiveness.

"What do you want of me?" she cried.

No voice came back. Or did it? Had she heard an answer, or did she just *wish* she had? Did she want an answer so strongly that her mind constructed one?

Wrapped it up in a bow, just for her, and spake it from an imagined mouth? *Perhaps I've gone insane.*

"Speak up," she tried again. "If you dare, answer me."

"*I dare*," whispered.

Rose recoiled at the voice, but upon searching saw no one. "Then speak, and be it the truth, for nothing else will serve either of us."

"*I thought my purpose clear.*"

"Well it is not. Make it so."

"*I wish to prevail myself upon thee, to fornicate with every man. My need has now become thine own.*"

"To what end?"

"*I crave the seed of man. It is my sustenance. I cannot survive without it.*"

"And I should care for your wellbeing?"

"*Thy concern is overwhelming, I'm sure. But my need is now thy need...OUR need. It is already too late.*"

"And if I resist you?"

"*Thou cannot!*" it answered, forcefully.

At that moment, Rose felt something pull within her. A physical tug on her mind that drove her to delirium, she could not help but thrust her hands between her legs as she had behind her own desk only days before. She focused on the spot that would quickly satisfy her need. But the urge continued. She could not stop, as had been the case before.

"No!" She willed her hands away. They swooned back. She buried them beneath the pillow.

Again they returned to their lustful duty. She locked them behind her back and laid her body on top. They wiggled and squirmed their way out and went back to work. Finally she rose and began her chores, neglected for days. For a moment she had won.

"There, I told you."

If she expected a response, it disappointed her. For a few minutes she managed to scrub dishes. But as soon as she turned to her next duty, her hands returned to theirs. Soon she fell to the floor and rolled into the wonderful feelings her fingers created, knowing rawness and pain would follow soon enough. The beast had won.

"What must I do to make this stop?"

"Thou can do nothing. Our need is strong. Have I not told thou it is too late?"

Rose believed. At that moment she knew not the path of salvation.

"You want what?"

"Can you do it?"

"Of course. But such a thing, what could it possibly be used for?"

"For that which it is intended."

"But why? Surely in Hemmingforth, such a thing would serve no purpose. It would be obsolete."

"I have the money to pay. I work for the office of the Magistrate. I say there is a need for a metal chastity belt that can be locked. I'd prefer you did not question further, as the Magistrate has said this thing is to be kept secret. No one is to know."

Rose thought hard about how she wanted the man to simply believe her words. She focused, hoping the determination in her eyes would convince him further than mere words. When she saw his head lift, a new look had taken over his face.

"You say you want it when?"

"How soon can you..." She paused. "Is there something wrong?" Then she felt the tug, once again. Not the same as she had at home, but similar enough for her to recognize its origins. The thing wanted more. She turned to leave.

"Wait."

She turned back.

"What about my payment?"

Perhaps because she recognized her possession, or for some other reason, but she knew her opportunity to retreat had passed. Her urge, combined with whatever power she'd exerted on the blacksmith, mingled to make an irresistible drive. She would resist no longer. Until she had everything ready, she remained at the mercy of the demon inside her.

She walked with the man to the back of the building where shadows lay like thick blankets on the ground. She dropped her dress and began the task of untying only enough knots to allow her petticoat to fall. Rose couldn't remember ever having bothered, but she now thought about how she'd have to clean her undergarment once again.

As the smith's eyes roamed over her nude form, she felt admired and adored. But she wished he would dispense with the pleasantries and get to work. She needed him inside her, offering his seed. She stepped forward.

With his pants around his ankles, trying to step backwards, he fell over, banging his head hard on the floorboards. He shook it several times but didn't appear to clear it. Rose, exasperated, pushed his head all the way back down against the floor once again. She looked at his manhood, ready for her, waving in the wind like a flagpole.

She had no time to waste while he found his sight. She straddled him and sat, taking him inside and closing her eyes. She moved like she was churning butter. Up and down, up and down, her legs grew tired and still she moved, pumping at him, pulling all the juice from him. But he had stamina and she continued.

Grabbing a post nearby, she kept her balance and moved herself faster. She knew he could hold out only so long and then she would receive that which it wanted. *She* wanted. She could hardly wait to feel it wash inside her, spraying deeper than any man could reach on his own—adding to the warmth of her already smoldering nether pot.

Now the man moved to compliment her efforts. His hips, made powerful by his constant work movement and carrying heavy objects, pounded against her, driving her off balance, bringing ecstasy. She finished and he still hadn't. Weakness entered her legs and they began to quiver with the exertion.

The man, seeing and understanding her plight, tossed her aside. She rolled over and lay on her back, exposed. He jumped on her, mounting like he would a steed, and rode her until she could feel pain in her back from the rough floor. Still he continued.

He rested his entire body on her, his powerful arms enwrapped her and squeezed tightly. Unable to get air, she began to swoon. When she felt consciousness slip away, she also felt him empty his wanton desire into her. She couldn't control another outburst of her own need before passing out.

When she woke, the smith had returned to work at the front of his shop. She dressed and walked out. His eyes refused to meet hers, even though she stared at him sharply. She watched his arms for a moment as he worked the red-hot metal into whatever shape he desired. She admired his work…and his arms.

"My piece?"

"What?"

"The work I asked for?"

"Oh, that. I can have it for you by tomorrow." He glanced around to make sure no one overheard. "Have you got a way to get it home?"

"I have not. Can you deliver it? Then I can pay you."

He whispered. "I think you paid me enough. Something like that at Madame Chatterwell's would have cost twice as much as the piece you require."

Again Rose's dark nature took over. "I'm sure there's a little more where that came from, just to make it worth your while. Call it a *delivery fee*."

The smith coughed and wiped his mouth with the back of a gloved hand. Not all his sweat came from the heat of the coal urn, she surmised. Although she would be rid of this demon, she could not help but admire the power she still wielded over a man. She strode out under a warm sun.

The smith came as he promised, and as the demon within Rose demanded. This time the man had little trouble mounting her. She led him to the bedroom and never even turned on her charm. The simplicity of not resisting seemed enough. The man's animal drives took over and she found herself falling onto her bed.

He dove in with fury and lust—two of Rose's favorite things. He kissed her, in several places. She did not resist. He touched things she'd never touched.

She did not resist. He tried to enter her in all her openings. She did not resist. He reached more than one peak and wanted more. Still, she did not resist.

Rose moved for him, into him, with him, dancing the whore dance. She cared not for lady status, as long as the men kept coming—coming back for more. The demon had spoken the truth. She needed it. The seed, the juice, the essence of man, the elixir of procreation, she wanted it all to fill her. At that moment, while this lone man wildly tossed her about and used her so roughly, she wished for the dream where more than one man slipped inside her at the same time.

If he read her mind, she hadn't been aware of it. And yet he rolled her over and took her in a different opening. Face down; she felt his pelvis against her buttocks, pounding her into the mattress. She felt pain and pleasure and buried her scream into the bed beneath. Her eyes crossed as another special moment erupted from her body and the spots he touched.

Finally exhausted and spent, he fell off her and rolled away. Whether embarrassed or simply finished and returning to work, she knew not—and cared not. He'd treated her to some incredible feelings, and he'd brought the object of her desire. Of all things, this one man, this smith, had been like a going away present, given to the demon by Rose. It knew not her plan…yet. But she offered it one last Harrah.

The smith left and she realized she did not even know his name. A laugh escaped her lips as she stood and examined the device. It looked perfect and she donned it with ease, locking it after she placed it proper. The ping of the lock bolt snapping into place made her heart jump.

Wearing only metal underpants, she put on a pot of water to boil and searched for a dress—just the right dress, one that would hide her new undergarment. When the water boiled she picked up the pot, took several deep breaths, and poured the liquid down the front of the chastity belt—scalding the tender flesh of her womanhood.

Rose screamed. When the pain subsided, she dressed and left to find Wilford.

Behind his desk, Wilford looked more like a judge than ever. Rose had been two days without showing up to work. She thought he might be cross but found him in complete disarray from concern for her wellbeing.

"I thought something might have happened to you. Something, terrible."

"I am all right. Would you keep something for me?"

"What is it?"

She handed him a solitary key. The lonely object fell into his outstretched hand with a nearly silent thud. He cupped it reverently, examined it curiously, and then clutched it affectionately. His eyes, full of questions, rose to meet hers.

"And what is this?"

"A key."

"As I can see. To what, may I ask?"

"Shall we just say it is a key to my heart? Sufficient answer under the circumstances, I should think."

"Please don't be so short with me, darling. I only care what happens to you. Would that we could be married this very day."

"A pleasant thought, my dear. Please hold it close to your heart even as you would hold this key. Both may soon unlock a love stronger than any other."

"But will you not stay and speak with me?"

"I cannot. I must go."

"For how long?" Wilford sounded quite desperate.

"I shall only need a couple days, I think."

"After that?"

"I shall return. I promise."

"And what of the time in between? How shall I ever contain myself?"

"Please believe in my love for you. One way or another, I shall return." She stood.

"Must you go this instant?"

"I...left a pot of water boiling on the stove."

With that she stepped out the door and did not look back.

The afternoon bore on and the water boiled. She could hardly stand the metal touching against her scorched flesh. She could not sit. She could not stand. She could definitely not walk. All things hurt. And yet she persisted, pouring one pot of scalding water after another down her front. Each time she screamed. Each time the pain subsided…a little. Each time she composed herself, she felt the urge to laugh.

She would laugh at the demon. Sooner or later, she *would* laugh at it. With the protection of the belt and the scarred skin, no one would have need to touch her ever again. Wilford would understand. *He has to.* She could not allow this to go further. The demon must go. No exorcism would be enough. No priest or judge would understand her despair.

"Thou mustn't."

"Be silent. Your time is nearly over. I'm sure you know I can't be dissuaded. I've already scalded myself to disfigurement. No man will ever again find me attractive down there. I may no longer be able to bear children. I may not even find pleasure in my own hands from this day forth. But here and forever more, shall be of my choosing. I choose." She poured yet another pot of water down, bringing her screams as she fell to her knees. When it passed, she lifted her head proudly. "Ha!"

"*I am beaten. How can this be? Thou art but human. And the desire already existed within thine heart. I had but to touch the right places.*"

"You did and I served you. If you had asked for but a short time I would have been what you need. But you ask forever and I shall have my own life returned. I cannot follow your path, no matter how tempting, or how pleasurable."

"*But I loved thee, Rose.*"

"Love? You don't know what the word means. You think that little game men and women play is love? It is simply an expression of love. So who is this superior being? You are a *mere* demon—beneath me. One such as you could never understand the complexities of love."

She checked the water which had nearly reached boil once again. After the first couple times of throwing water on her floor, she discovered a quicker, cleaner way. She took a second pot and placed it beneath her on the floor. It caught most of the water poured and retained some of the heated temperature. After hours, this became quite efficient.

"*Perhaps I could not understand human love. But I offered something greater. I could have offered thee—.*"

"Do not presume to be so magnanimous. You are not a savior. You are not God. You have no magnificence to offer. There is no salvation in your words, only sorrow. You could bring me nothing but eternal damnation. One wanton sexual encounter after another, deeper into depravity, perhaps with women or children, multiple partners, animals, to what depths you would not sink I am uncertain, and in the end you would be stronger and I would be burning for an eternity in Hell. We have no future together. I give you leave to depart at any time."

Again the water heralded its arrival to temperature. She poured, she screamed, she returned the pot to the stove. For a time her mind remained quiet. It could have been gone, but she knew it wasn't. She could feel it nearby, breathing heavily as if injured and dying. She maintained her vigil as long as she could past nightfall, then fell to her bed—exhausted. She didn't even mind the scent of the act she'd performed with the smith, clinging to her comforter and sheets. She knew she might never smell it again. Rose passed out and did not dream.

Upon waking, she began her pattern once again. Water boiled, water poured. Scream, knees, repeat. The demon's heartbeat, if indeed it had a heart, resounded in her ears, keeping her wary of its presence. She knew it was not far away.

Her vigil lasted all that day and into the next night, where again she fell into a dreamless sleep. Stopping seemed pointless. When she awoke, she began again, continuing for a third day. Her screams abated as the skin became desensitized. Then she would pour more water and realized it might still be more sensitive than she thought. She screamed again.

By that night she began to falter. Her resolve faded and she wondered how long the demon could hold out. She could certainly not maintain this for weeks, if it took that long. Even a couple more days seemed more than she could endure. She decided a confrontation might best resolve the problem once and for all.

"Show yourself," she said with a weak voice.

Nothing came back to her. She doubted her senses.

"I know you're still there."

Nothing.

Could she possibly have gotten rid of it and not noticed? Her aloneness struck her. Solitude—not exactly a lifestyle chosen by most women—had once offered her solace. Now it seemed more antagonizing, taunting, teasing her about the pathetic life she now led.

Perhaps the beast had left her, too. But this time she would choose not to remain alone.

"Rose! Are you well?" Wilford's concern showed all over his morning face. Stubble from a forgotten morning ritual sparkled with the beams of sun that shone through the wall boards. Dust fairies floated about, dancing when anyone walked through them. Her gait, pained and distorted, gave him cause for concern, but she pooh-poohed it away with a wave of her hand.

"I am perhaps not so terrible as I might appear. Are you well?" she asked, sliding one weak palm across his unshaven cheek.

"Sleep has evaded me. I have waking dreams of some terror devouring you, bite by bite, and casting your bones aside with nothing left on them but spittle. I hear your voice in the night, but it does not offer words of love, it cries out for help. Finally, unable to bear it further, I trod to your house in the dark and fell back on the front porch, awaiting your emergence. When the time came and the sun persistently stabbed at my eyes, I rose and came here, hoping this is the one place you would go when ready. And here you are."

"Here I am, my love. I have returned as promised."

"And so you have. I am so sorry that I should have ever doubted you."

"I can understand your concerns, and your doubts. But lay them to rest now."

"You are such an angel. How have I lived so long without you?"

"I have no answer for that, my love. But I assure you, there is no reason to live any longer without

117

me. Nor I, without you. I care not for opinion; I will wed you as soon as you see fit to have me."

"Even if that were today?"

"Even so. I've known of my love for quite some time. Hiding it behind lies and denial cannot possibly be more Christian than a hasty wedding. Such a desire, filling my heart, taking my every thought, is that not lust? I would take that away, cast it out."

"What of your…demon."

"It is gone."

"Gone?"

"I have eliminated its hold over me, therefore it is powerless. I am free of it."

"Can you be sure it will never return?"

"Can any of us?"

"True," he said, glancing toward his desk. "There is a past of which I am embarrassed and would bury. Would that anyone could accept it and forgive."

"I can."

"But you know not."

"Perhaps I do."

"But how?"

"As you knew of my antics. I oversaw something I should not have. And yet, here we both are, together, professing our love. Perhaps it is all for the best. Now we can go forward without secrets."

Wilford smiled. Her words struck him true, and warmed him.

Rose felt relief knowing he knew about her past. She didn't know how much he knew, but she, of course,

118

did not know all there was to know about his past, either. When time had passed and they grew ever more comfortable with each other, they could speak further— if they chose to do so. For now, enough was known. Except…

"There is one further thing I must confess, even now at the infancy of our relationship."

"You needn't bother, my love."

"I must."

"Why must you?"

"It cannot wait, I assure you. Would that I could put it off, but your decision may hinge on this truth as much as many others—perhaps more so. Once known, you may choose to abandon me."

He slid his arms around her and she felt so safe and comforted. "There could never be anything that would make me turn from you."

"Perhaps." She stood and paced a bit, unable to find the strength to continue. She feared his retribution. She feared he would leave. But to hide it until after a ceremony that tied him to her until death—that would be dishonorable and downright mean. She could not. She sought to explain, but could not find the words. She would have to show all.

"My love, I will need the key I asked you to hold."

"Is your heart no longer to be mine?"

"Perish the thought. My heart beats for naught but you. The need for my own life pales."

"It does not...to me." He pulled at his neck, producing a chain. Hanging from it she saw the key that had helped her rid herself of the demon. He'd kept it close to his own heart for safe keeping.

He held out the key now but she did not take it right away. She tried to raise her dress but its bulk kept falling back. She struggled for a moment and gave up. Reaching behind, Rose began untying the draw strings that held the garment in place.

"What are you doing?"

"Patience, my love."

"But you cannot undress in here. What if someone were to walk in?"

"I have locked the door behind me. No one will enter." Then the dress fell to the floor. Unable to fit a petticoat over the chastity belt, Rose stood naked except for it. Wilford stared. To his credit, he did not but casually glance at her bare breasts. However his curiosity drew his gaze to the metallic object attached to her hips.

"What is that?"

"A chastity belt."

"Chastity? But you..." He trailed off.

"I know what you saw. No matter the desire in my heart or the past of my life, this was a demon."

"I know. I saw your eyes."

"My eyes?" She thought about it and decided she did not want to know. "Never mind. The demon seemed to work through my womanhood, so I locked it out."

"Indeed? Such a wise solution." His voice carried genuine admiration.

"But there is more. A lock will not a demon keep out, of itself. I needed to further deter the beast that sought to control me—to bar its return. I needed to act swiftly before my will was lost forever."

"Again your wisdom is impressive. I am so lucky to have fallen in love with such an intelligent girl."

"Perhaps you will not think so when you see." As she spoke she struggled with the temperamental lock. Finally it fell away and the belt slipped easily off. Wilford got his first glimpse of her tortured nether area, as did Rose.

The rotting flesh, red with anger and blistered, stared at them both. No hair remained and all of her could be seen. The flesh down there could not withstand the torture she'd put it through. Had she chosen a place with toughened skin, as on her hands, it might not have looked so. Wilford turned away.

"It will heal."

"I know." His weakened answer struck her as a hand on her face.

"It seemed the only way."

"You may be right," he said, turning back, "for I have never heard of anyone removing their own demon before. You may very well be the first. And I promise you, when you have healed, I will learn to overlook the scars you have. For do we not all have scars from

121

battle? The deepest of which are from those fought with ourselves." He moved close to her.

"Indeed they are."

"How did you manage?"

"Boiling water."

"Ah," he offered. "It could have been so much worse."

"I see not how."

He placed his hand gently on the tortured flesh between her legs. She winced, but did not withdraw. "This is a place of hiding—only I shall see from this day forth." He looked into her eyes. "That is true, is it not?"

"Only you, my love."

He relaxed and allowed a smile to lift one corner of his mouth. "Worse would have been on your face or somewhere everyone could see. No one ever need know of this."

"Should we lie?"

"A lie of omission. Surely no decent person would ask such a question."

"That is a truth I had not thought of," she answered with a tilt of her head. "But the question of marriage remains. What if I cannot bear you children?"

"In my many years of training, I was required to study the human body. From what I know, most of what you need to bring forth a child is inside. Unless you stood on your head and poured scalding water directly inside, I think children are not out of the question. The only question is how soon you will have healed enough for us to act as man and wife in this manner."

Now it was Rose's turn to smile. If only he could be telling the truth. But then, why would he not? Nothing could be gained by his falsehood. And only he would lose if she could not bear children. Yet he persisted.

"Then we shall proceed with the plans for a wedding. I shall announce it today."

"Shall we go right now, Wilford? Shall we?" Her childlike excitement could hardly be contained and she turned toward the door.

"I think…" he began. She frowned at his hesitation. "…we could wait for you to dress first."

She looked down and giggled. It wouldn't do her already tarnished reputation any good to go out in such an array. "I'll have to go without anything underneath. I brought nothing and I cannot don that terrible thing again."

Wilford kicked the metal bucket to the side. "Pray God you never again have to wear this device. We shall place it on our mantle as a reminder."

"But it is not proper for me to walk about freely with nothing under my dress."

"Yes, people might think you've become promiscuous…on your way to announce plans for matrimony."

They both laughed.

Few people attended the wedding. Though held in church, the pastor could find no comfort sanctioning such a union. God, he said, did not approve of unholy joinings. Her past and his uncertain beginnings would be exposed someday. God would not allow such things to remain hidden from the eyes of the righteous for long.

Rose laughed at the 'eyes of the righteous' comment. She knew many of the people in town. She felt little concern for the tainting of righteousness. Men lured by the demon's lust could easily be discounted, and perhaps forgiven, but many men had visited Rose when she led that life—without a demon's influence—having no remorse for their lustful acts. Why should she be the only one to bear the burden of sin? Had they not sinned as well?

Despite all the judgment against her, and the poor gathering of people to celebrate her special day, Rose stood tall and proud, enjoying the moment as much as any woman ever did. More, perhaps. And she would not let the foolish minds of the 'righteous' darken the few bright clouds that floated in the sky above her.

To her, all was as it should be. She went to her home with Wilford and began a life she knew would be happy for eternity. Though her scars faded in the weeks that followed, Wilford would not have relations with her unless the room was totally darkened. Rose needed no lights and, although it pained her heart, considered it a small price to pay.

The first time he tried to enter her, the pain kept her from fulfilling his needs. She could have nothing touch her there and often slept in the nude without covers. But she soon grew tolerant and could accept him as she had any man. After a time she even began to enjoy his advances and thought she might someday return to her old self, finding pleasure and release in the act. She longed for that.

In the meantime, she allowed Wilford his own pleasures and shared in his satisfaction. Each time he gave his seed, she felt more like the lady she sought to be. She was still wanton, but only with him. And under God, this was not a sin since they were married proper.

And every night Rose prayed for herself and for Wilford, that they might have a long and Christian life together, under the watchful eye of God. She prayed they be accepted by the town. And she prayed for healing—both physical and emotional. She also prayed that Wilford find true happiness in her—both physically and emotionally. And she prayed for children.

The world became a wonder for Rose. Her wanton urges subdued, the growing relationship with

Wilford, a job to produce money, all these lent way to a level of happiness she'd not known. Though pride be one of the seven deadly sins, she could not keep it from her heart. She felt it about her marriage and home. She felt it about her victory over evil. And now she could feel it for the budding life growing within her. Wilford had been right. She could still bear children.

She walked with a bounce, unaware of the evil that still watched her every move, stalking each step, waiting for strength and opportunity. Rose trod as a lady but the evil messenger knew her true nature as being one of a lust that flowed through her as much as the seed of man. With ease she held at bay the desire to taste each one as they passed. And even though such desires were not entirely purged, she fought with the natural feelings of turmoil within her. The doctor told her that womanly urges sometimes became greater during pregnancy. She would have to live with it—and resist.

The beast knew this would move to weaken her even as it grew stronger. As it planned its own return, the hellspawn lay casually in the undeveloped bosom of another younger girl, seeking, desiring, collecting. Wanting, needing only the seed; rich and vitalizing, to quench its need and produce offspring.

But Rose, despite her darkened past, was innocent. She knew not the world and nature, nor of things unnatural and other-worldly. The Sunday sermons told her all she knew of the afterlife, be it dark or light; fire or sunshine. And the first time the demon

126

appeared in her mirror, she dismissed the image as dark fancy—frightening, to be sure, but nothing more than smoke.

She spoke not of it to neighbors for fear of retribution. But inside, she knew it had been there and remembered what it looked like. If only she could know why it appeared to her. By mid-fall, she had caught glimpses of the image all of eleven times. The latter ones becoming longer and more difficult to so easily deny. One day in early October she spoke to Wilford about it through trembling lips.

"I've seen it several times, my lord."

Wilford knew when she spoke so formally, she feared his reaction. This he'd learned in a short time as her tone often told of her true feelings. This moment, he could tell by the quiver in her voice, would have to be handled in a most delicate fashion.

"Do you recognize it? What did it look like?"

"A horrible creature. Like nothing I've ever seen or heard tell of."

"Did it hurt you?"

"No, but I was terribly frightened."

"Indeed, as well you should have been. It does not sound holy."

"You think me mad, or possessed."

"Be still," he spoke softly, touching her gently. "Hush. I think no such thing. But it is difficult to believe without having seen it with mine own true eyes."

"Knowing is not the same as hearing, but you must believe. Hear with your heart. I speak the truth. And I know not what to do," she broke into a sob.

"There," he coddled her.

Rose gathered her mettle and stood fast against Wilford's doubt.

"What must I do?"

"Without knowing what it wants, we may have no recourse. May it be that you could find out?"

"How would I accomplish such a feat?"

"This from the woman who eradicated it all by herself the last time it dared approach.

"You think it the same demon, then?"

"What other?"

"So how do I set about discovering its purpose?"

"You might...ask."

"Just come out and inquire about its intention? I hardly think that's an appropriate method of addressing a true demon."

"Perhaps it simply wants to reenter you."

"As do many men, I'm sure," she said, not without sarcasm. "But that time has passed."

"A time will come when its true goals shall be known. For us to bend to its eventual will dictates we must know."

"I do not understand, my husband."

"For any slave to obey his master, he must be made aware of the rule of law. What will make his master happy? What makes him cross? And what are the punishments for disobedience?"

"So you believe it will *want* to tell me?"

"Perhaps. Subterfuge can be difficult to see through. We must remain hopeful."

"Somehow it seemed much easier to stand against when inside me."

"Probably because you could not lay eyes on its evil form. Fright has taken some of your strength. You must regain it. Remember this is a demon you already bested."

Rose slumped, an unattractive gesture to be sure. Nevertheless, the weight of burden pressed down upon her and she sought refuge. Something within told her she could stand and face the creature and yet fear overwhelmed. She could not remember life being so difficult when she lived it as she had. Hunting for men to offer that which they secretly sought was no burden at all. All she need do was maintain an attractiveness that could still lure.

The time would come in her future, as with any woman, when appearances would fail and the body—falter. She knew such things to be inevitable. But one so young as Rose did not fully believe in the inevitability of aging, even as her body began to grow with child.

Life, however, had taken an unexpected turn and she wanted to be with Wilford. This concept left no room for promiscuity. She'd mended her ways only to discover newer, taller obstacles to overcome. Rose felt sadness because she knew other adults would rather turn tail and run than face such terror. She envied them.

Somewhere within, she must locate a deep strength. She drew so much from Wilford, but knew this battle had to be won by her and her alone. She must call upon the desire to be rid of the demon. She must find it if she were to live.

Winter had fallen and an evil pursued her. Rose ran toward home, toward Wilford—for he would surely be there. *But perhaps it would be unwise to lead it to him and have him share my fate.* She sought to change direction. *The stables would smell of comfort,* she thought without knowing why. To her dismay her feet had not done as she'd commanded of them. She still ran full speed toward home, and him.

She recited the Lord's Prayer over and over again through puffed breathes.

Her feet slowed, not at all, but her mouth came to an abrupt halt. Rose had the feeling of not being alone yet no one stood near. The sparse trees accented by white snow would go far to expose any who might skulk as a thief. Such a barren landscape could hide naught but the winter-white rabbit even as twilight fell heavy upon her.

However, the feeling of a companion persisted, haunted. She turned to and fro in search but her eye caught nothing. Her foot, oppositely, caught very good hold of a strong and still-green pine root that jutted up in a most inconvenient manner.

Rose went down, her mouth poised to scream, quickly filled with fresh, dusty snow. Her body heat, raised by the exertion of the run, melted the snow in her mouth almost instantly. She drank as she assessed herself for injury.

"Thou art unharmed."

The voice sang in Rose's ear and she looked around, focusing into the depths of darkness hiding behind every tree, growing deeper as the sun sank further beneath the horizon. Her stomach fluttered from the fear—renewed. Her voice, when she spoke, quivered with uncertainty.

"Who's there?"

The wind answered with a low growl that sounded quite out of natural and Rose shivered against more than just cold. She gathered back to her feet and stopped still, as in shock, when the voice danced through her head, once again.

"Thou should hurry home, child."

Rose listened close to the voice within her ears that seemed to come from nowhere and yet lingered as the scent from a stew pot.

"Make haste, thy husband awaits."

Rose set out again at full gallop, this time watching closely as her feet pounded the earth—propelling her at a speed she'd never experienced. As she ran she wished herself to greater speed though she knew the futility. Her legs began to ache and she knew her time of running would soon come to an end.

Then, she saw the light splash against the snow from the windows of her own home. The figure. It stood fast in puddles of melted snow beneath its feet. Heat from the body created steam, floating like an early-morning mist that gathered about it as if by choice. It stood between her and the door.

At first, believing it to be Wilford, Rose pushed her way forward. Now, as her eye approached and vision cleared to see the truth, she faltered. Although arreptitious, she stood to ponder and examine.

The apparition before her stood as she did. Arms protruded from its shoulders and the body turned almost as if in pain. The scream which sprung from it would confirm that. But the horrible noise turned into a sound to frighten even more. One might call it a laugh. Rose shivered.

Before her eyes the thing faded and she saw her own doorstep become visible through it. When it fully dissipated she made her way through the door, slamming it behind her. She found the house, however, devoid of life save her own. Wilford must have stepped out for some reason.

Feeling the fear grow she made her way to the bedroom. An ache stung at her and she made way to examine. Some pains came from areas she could not easily see and she made her way to her large mirror, but her reflection faded even as the demon had moments ago. What took its place stole her breath.

Its misshapen head turned to her and it glared with fire-filled eyes. Arms with a half dozen joints each, jiggled and twisted—legs with no knees hobbled with weight first on one then the other—the beast looked as though it were trying to dance through fire and agony.

At some point—Rose had lost any real sense of time—the thing peeled back its mucous lips in a hideous mock smile—though the rotted stubs protruding inside that mouth could hardly be called teeth.

Swollen areas on the chest (could those be breasts?) raised as it sucked in air. A viscous fluid—the color of watered-down milk—dripped from each one. Finally, it spoke and the voice grated like the bay of a horse with a broken leg. It said only one word.

"*Rose!*"

Rose cringed from it as if its breath came putrid and she could smell through the glass. Digging from deep within she found the fortitude to reply.

"What art thou?"

"*I am called* Beelzertft. *I am a succubus.*"

"What would that be?" Rose spoke with uncertain austerity.

"*I come for the babies.*" Something about the voice seemed confrontational, daring her to inquire

133

further. She glanced down at her slightly protruding belly.

"No babies have been born here for many months. You attempt to deceive."

"*I do not. The babies have been provided.*"

Confused, Rose looked about; searching for the strength she counted on, the name of her power. Wilford. But he would not be found. She could not fathom where he'd gotten to when she needed him so.

"*Worry not for him, child. But mourn over thine own self for truly thy soul be lost.*"

"You will not have me or my baby."

"*I need not thy baby. The seed thou hast drawn from the men of this town hast given me many babies. Thou art their mother.*"

"No!"

"*Thou art the new Eve. Together we could bring forth a whole new world.*"

"I will not give in to your temptations. I have a life now."

"*What life? As a mere woman? Thou hast the same life as any mortal. Is that all thou aspires to?*"

"I will not be drawn in!" she shouted.

The creature in the mirror withdrew slightly.

The arrival of Wilford heralded a lifting. 'Twere as if a knife had been withdrawn from her back or shackles removed from her limbs. Rose stood tall and strong against the power she faced.

"'Tis said no weapon of God's Earth can destroy the beast but spiritual purity wilt surely cast it out!" Wilford's voice carried above the din.

"I am not pure," Rose confessed. "Thou knowest."

"True, perhaps, but thy God is. He is there to take on the fight in your behalf, if you only let Him."

"What of our baby?"

"God will nurture the innocents. You need not fear."

"I know so little of such things, Wilford." Yet her feet didst move forward again, but human strength alone could not stand against the supernatural.

"You must have faith, my darling." Wilford spoke softly yet his voice still carried. His words, nay his *one* word; *darling*, caressed her ears.

Rose felt more powerful than ever. Her heart sang and she *knew* if she survived, she and Wilford would be together for eternity. The joy of first seeing him on the street that day came into her that moment, creating a renewed purity. The pureness of dawning love, true love, untainted by anger or lust, as she felt it that morning.

God moved through her as she thrust out her hands. No force seen of the eye flowed from her yet the beast withdrew as if in pain. With her heart light and her mind focused only on the task, she never so much as diverted her eyes. All was for *Beelzertft*.

Blood flowed from its eyes even as the screech came out of its hideous mouth. The claw-like hands spasmed, trying to grasp at salvation. Naught would help. The power of Rose became more than it could stand against.

　　With a final scream that turned into a cackle, the apparition faded into the mists of dimming memory, leaving Wilford unsure of its demise. Rose slumped and he rushed to catch her. She managed to reach her destination on the floor before he could encompass her with his arms and lift. He picked her up to rest on one squatted knee. Stroking her hair from her face, Wilford softly called to her.

　　Moments stretched in Wilford's mind as thoughts of the worst came to him. Yet she stirred with pained effort and managed, after some coaxing, to open her eyes. As she beheld the object of her love, a smile crept weakly to her lips. She opened her mouth to speak but *Beelzertft's* voice came.

　　"Beware. Evil may be abated but ever shall it return. My time is nigh as this visit has foretold. Be thou prepared if thy wishes. But I say unto thee, I shall have my due, be ye prepared or otherwise. And no amount of sweetness will force me hence."

　　Wilford stared.

"My love, why dost thou look at me so?" came Rose's innocent query.

"Didst you not hear? The beast spake from your very mouth," he added, touching her lips with his fingers.

Shocked, she inquired further. "What didst thou hear, my beloved?"

"It foretold of its return and warned we would not be able to sto—."

Susann's fingers gripped at the tender flesh beneath Wilford's chin. She lifted him even as she stood. He looked at her in puzzlement. She returned his gaze with the eyes of the underworld. A fire burnt deep within those eyes. Wilford recognized the demon look from the day of the picnic and feared.

She held him with only one hand, his feet unable to touch the floor, as she called upon the strength of the unnatural one. Evil, in its own right, didst have strength over mortal man. It could not easily be denied. Her other hand slid intimately down the front of him. She reached the object which she sought and freed it.

Stroking him in such a manner made him recoil. Arousal, though, seemed involuntary. A smile fell upon Rose's face when the beast within saw his reaction. Even as Wilford's life ebbed—her one hand continuing to keep pressure on his throat—myriad thoughts ran through his head, but he drew only one to the front. *How will I live without her?*

The short-bladed sword he always carried—although hidden not to cause undo fear—came easily from its sheath. A family heirloom, the blade swung in a perfect, almost beautiful arc, contacted the neck of the woman Wilford loved. An eternity in the moment, he considered that he would never cry into that neck, nor find any comfort there from a gentle embrace. Their children would never nuzzle as they burped, freshly taken from her breast. He would never hang a necklace from that neck—bought perhaps for her birthday. And he would never kiss her there as they made love in their bed—in their home.

The finely-honed blade hesitated for naught. Through the neck, it slowed little and the swing carried it over and pulled it from Wilford's hands. The blade dug firmly into the wall on the far side of the room.

Wilford wanted to hold the woman he'd loved so completely. Yet he feared. The hands clutched in death spasms, gripping at his arms, squeezing and releasing—squeezing and releasing. Rose's chest heaved with unholy breaths. And a horrible sound emerged from the neck as if the imperishable beast continued to throw curses at him.

And so he dropped the headless body to the floor with a tear—it continued taunting him without the ability to form true words. Hardened by the tragedy the beast brought upon his home, he retrieved the sword then turned and left without uttering a word at her departure. No words spoken over the body would allow her into Heaven, or him. Mounting his horse, he rode toward town.

Was this to be my penance all along? God, thou hast truly forsaken me. Hers was the purest love, the bravest soul. Did she deserve to die? She carried my child. Was that the reason? She needed to die because she carried a child born of my seed? Am I evil so dark? God! Answer me! Was there no other way?

No answer came. His horse knew the way to town and stopped for nothing along the way. When soon the buildings appeared to him, he wondered how he could explain what he'd seen. The pastor would believe. He believed in evil. That was his job. Surely the Sheriff would be compassionate. They'd worked together and he knew Wilford to be a man of honor.

The horse carried him into town, but he didst not stop. No life there remained, not for him. With nary a backward glance, Wilford Denton Hemmingforth left the town and would not be heard of again in the village named after him.

In time, people chose a new name.

PRIDE AND PERDU

By:
Blue Canyon

The warm liquid shot into her. This sensation created more fear than anything else had so far—anything she could remember in her whole life. She had no protection. She didn't think she needed any. The evening should have been quiet and alone, she made no plans to be intimate with a man.

Darla couldn't explain a thing. Obviously a man, a man with a face that couldn't be seen, had found his way in—inside her apartment, inside her bedroom, inside her vagina.

He must have been there the whole time, since she got home from work. He would have seen her undress. He'd probably watched her shower, too. She masturbated in the shower. Further embarrassment washed over her.

He must have been there while she ate dinner and read the latest novel, *Steel Mill Mafia* by Al Musitano. Darla got quite engrossed in the gangster story that didn't read like a gangster story. She laughed and cried and cheered for the underdog. She couldn't be sure, but she thought she might have cheered out loud, once or twice.

Then, when she got up to slip into bed and try to sleep, she felt his strong hands grabbing her, pushing her robe off with ease. Exposed, she felt so much weaker and instantly forgot everything she'd been taught at the martial arts classes she'd taken almost a year before.

When he first grabbed her, she couldn't understand how she'd missed him for hours. But now, as he shot his sperm into her (like a fireman, he just keeps coming!), she knew the answer. She could see the ceiling above her bed. She could see right through him, as if he had no head. When she looked down she saw no body either. No arms held her tight. No ass bounced in the air above her. No penis that pumped gallons of baby batter into her aching pussy. An amusing thought tickled her brain. *Is his semen invisible, too?*

Despite seeing nothing, her legs were forced wide open. She could feel that penis, rubbing against the inside walls of her womanhood. She could feel his eruption inside. The weight of his body lay on top of her. Something she couldn't see—some *man* she couldn't see—raped her, came inside her, and quite probably impregnated her. *Pregnancy. That would be the worst.* Fear washed over her like an ocean wave.

His throbbing *something* slid in and out of her, rubbing her, mixing her fear and disgust with desire and ecstasy. Her heightened emotions and his continued movement had her nearly at a peak, but the splash of his fluid inside sent her into an unexpected orgasm.

Her nipples tightened painfully. She thrust her head back and squeezed her eyes shut, hoping she looked to be in pain. She didn't want to give the impression she enjoyed any part of this, despite her body's reaction. Darla noticed her inner muscles gripping him—milking him—and she felt as transparent as her attacker. Then suddenly, silence. She could feel his weight still on her, but he'd stopped moving—stopped gushing into her.

When he got up, a part of her felt empty. She never saw him leave. She never saw anything—as if he was the invisible man. If she got caught by his seed, would she give birth to an invisible child?

He went away but Darla just lay there sobbing, her hands quivering, sweat and bodily fluids dripping down—following the crack of her ass to the mattress, tears flowing out of her eyes.

I can barely find my car keys, when I need them. How will I ever keep track of an invisible child?

Girls

By:
Blue Canyon

The moment came and so did I
When I saw the twinkling in her eye
I hadn't so much as removed my pants
Yet my breath came in short pants.

I stood behind to feel her breasts
As we hid in the closet, full of zest
Her zeal and pleasure were matched by none
As my hands explored her nipples, having fun.

Her back so soft and muscles fine
From my lips escaped a whine
Her little lace panty clung to her ass
My hands shook, I didn't want to move too fast.

The girl had curves that wouldn't quit
We made some noise, I frankly didn't give a shit
My penis rose hard, so I let it out.
When she saw she gasped, nearly a shout.

I knelt behind, kissing her derriere so sweet
As I dropped her panties to her feet
She tasted fine from the back side
And I spread her cheeks really wide.

Then I stood again, preparing to thrust
To enter the girl, fulfilling my lust
When I reached around in front to my shock
As I gripped the girl's full erect—and larger than mine—cock!

CYCLE OF

THE MOON

By:
Blue Canyon

The new moon, shadowed by Earth, watched over the hordes like a closed eye. The noise and lights of the carnival assured that no one would notice, so the moon hung in lonely silence above.

Howard Payne sat at the half podium, waiting for the lines of curious and morbid to pay their eight bits and enter the macabre trailer. The view inside— one of horror unseen in normal life—drew in the mundane who searched for a thrill to awaken the miserable adventurer within.

Denied such pleasures in his own life, Payne stole excitement vicariously from those partaking of the festivities. The thrill of a clown juggling fiery baseball bats, the fright of a distorted reflection in a bent mirror, a breathtaking drop from a roller coaster peak, all these gave the illusion of life to the otherwise lifeless.

He turned, examining once again, the words painted on the side of the trailer.

SEE THE HEADLESS WOMAN WHO STILL LIVES!

Beneath that, the image of a woman—a beautiful, voluptuous woman—in a red dress, laying on the ground, writhing in pain, her head removed and her neck bleeding her life away, and yet, somehow, not.

Payne thought the woman sexy, although he preferred his women taller. He hadn't been with a woman in a very long time. He travelled, wandered mostly, no job or town holding his interest for very long. Relationships took time, time he wouldn't waste on anyone or anything. With so much life waiting just around the next corner, he could not resist the call.

Still his loins, rooted in the weakness of man since time began, called for coupling—mating; the release of mortal urges to procreate. He felt *urge-ent* at that moment as he looked up and saw her standing—waiting.

Susan Sharpe stood nearly six-feet-tall. Looking down on other people had not been only in condescension for her. She offered Payne a fiery look, one that spoke to his urges—or was that just his imagination?

"May I help you?" he asked with a manly squeak.

She reached down and lifted the 'Help Wanted' sign, showing it to him. Payne, he abhorred being called 'Howie', looked at her incredulously.

"*You* want to work *here*?"

Susan said nothing, tipping the sign forward to draw his attention back to it.

"You *can* talk, can't you?"

"Of course."

Her syrupy voice poured over him, warm and clinging to his skin like liquid silk, nourishing the lust through his pores. He could feel tingling in his nether region. Discomfort grew inside and he squirmed in his chair. Under the podium lay a small stack of paper. From the bottom he withdrew one and handed it to the woman.

"This is a pre-app. Just fill it in and the owner," he cocked his thumb over his shoulder, "will call you."

She finished in seconds, coming around behind to hand it to him intimately. She leaned close and put her lips to his ear. Payne could hear her draw in a breath to speak.

"I'll be in…touch." Her finger slid down the side of his arm, stopping at his elbow, falling short of his lap where he hoped her hand would go.

Unable to calm his breathing, he responded with a simple grunt. He tried not to stare as she sashayed away, but no one would witness—no one could see— no one cared if he ogled. Several others eyed her movements as she walked.

Though it wouldn't be any of his concern, he studied her app, her handwriting, her signature. Susan Sharpe, a poetic name that rolled off the tongue like 'chocolate cake' or 'mint julep'. He savored the sound and longed for a taste.

He didn't have to wait long. That night, as he closed up, a hand touched him. He tried not to jump in fear. Still, he turned quickly.

"Susan! I mean, Ms. Sharpe. What brings you back here?"

She tilted her head to one side and ran her finger down his arm again. This time, she picked up his hand. Payne thought things couldn't get any better. Then she placed his hand on her C-cup breast.

He smiled. "Would you like to go back to my place?" He struggled not to stammer as he spoke.

She responded with a simple nod of her head. Her silky hair bounced gently with the movement. *A woman of few words. I could get used to that.*

Closing took too long, but fortunately his apartment wasn't far. She didn't stand on ceremony and immediately, upon entering his place, began to disrobe. After locking the door, Payne followed suit. Like most guys, he only wanted to wait because he thought that's what women wanted.

This woman, Susan Sharpe, didn't seem interested in typical social graces. She had a get-down-to-business attitude that Payne found quite refreshing.

Now, both nude, he embraced her, kissing passionately and exploring with his hands. She responded in kind. She wiggle-walked him toward the couch—not letting go of him—and fell, pulling him on top of her. She definitely didn't want to waste any time.

Entering her almost felt painful. He never considered himself well-hung, but this felt so tight he had trouble getting in. *She must not have been with many men.*

She wrapped him up tight in her arms and legs, not allowing him any more movement than was needed for the act they performed. She didn't want him taking his time, or changing positions, or doing anything other than pleasing her vagina.

So that's what he did. He held his orgasm off for as long as he could, hoping the extended motion would make up for all the other play he would have done but she hadn't given him the opportunity. Still, the entire incident lasted a very short time.

He remained on top of her, inside her, after everything had finished—draining, dripping. She appeared satisfied, but Payne couldn't be sure. Still, he felt a real attraction for this woman. He hated to think of love so soon, especially when a man felt love easily while in the throes of passion. Or right after.

She smelled so good and her comfortable smile suggested she had no plans to leave. He rolled next to her, his penis falling out of her pussy and laying against his leg, but never lost physical contact. Her skin electrified his entire body.

Before he fell asleep, he hoped he'd given her even half as much pleasure as she'd given him. Then the lights went out.

He woke alone, disappointed and a bit hurt, but not entirely surprised. She was an enigma. Work didn't start for several hours so he looked around for a note from her, just a sign that he hadn't dreamed it all, and that the feelings growing inside him weren't all one-way. By the time he had to leave, he'd found none.

Payne sat quietly at the podium, hoping she would show. The day passed with no sign of her. He looked forward to seeing her again with earnest, but a fortnight passed before she returned, apparently at the beckon of the owner. The smile embedded on her face told that she'd been hired. Payne tried looking into her eyes, hoping to find an explanation for her absence. She seemed to not notice him at all. His heart sank.

She disappeared into the motor home parked behind the trailer, Payne assumed for an interview. The hours passed, some people straggled in to see the anomaly in the trailer, but the girl never came back out.

The time arrived for Payne to close up, which the owners often left him to do on his own. He folded up shop, put away any paperwork and signs, and walked away, taking one last look back at the motor home.

His eye, drawn to the image on the side of the trailer, saw only sadness. He'd hoped to make a date with her when she exited. The image on the trailer he saw in his mind moved as if to draw him closer, he shook it off like dust in an attic.

Payne had only gone inside the trailer once when first hired. The headless body moved as if filled with life, trying to escape the terrible bonds that held it. He never wanted to see it again after that. It disturbed him and he hadn't slept for two nights following.

Sadness accompanied him home to his small apartment this night, haunting him with dreams of a night he could have had with Susan Sharpe, a night of unspeakable ecstasy. Perhaps the time for him to stay put for a while had finally arrived.

However, the next day saw no trace of her and Payne began to wonder if the opportunity for him to plant his root had truly come or if he should seek out other goals, and other potential mates.

As the day wore on, he tossed between wanting to forget and wanting to find the truth. He felt an interest in her and she'd obviously reciprocated. Somehow, he couldn't just leave another day without knowing what happened to her.

Hours progressed slowly and Payne felt a kind of madness temporarily sweep over him and he longed for the end of the day. His plan—search for her; find where the desire of his heart had gone. He wanted to know for sure he hadn't imagined her touch, or her scent.

Darkness fell and the crowds continued to fill the area. But the time to close arrived and people began leaving. Payne knew this process could take another hour, so he waited.

The time had come. He folded the doors and windows, bolting down the show, making it secure. During the day he'd been confused but knew one thing for sure. He decided where he'd begin his search.

The motor home parked out back.

He approached the run-down conversion truck with a touch of fear. The creepy, too-short couple that hired him made his stomach turn. And something inside made him sure they held truth in little regard.

Rather than face them even once more, Payne decided on a more clandestine approach. He peeked in one of the windows. He met with curtains and dim light, leaving him without any real proof of anything.

He climbed to a different window. A bit of light streamed out from a crack in the curtain and through this Payne forced his eye. He struggled but found if he turned just the right way, he could see almost the entire room.

On the floor, leather straps bolted through the metal bottom, held tight the woman Payne searched for. She lay nude, struggling. The man, Owen Scragg, knelt beside her, fondled her, his dirty smile made even uglier by the lust in his eyes.

Into the room waddled Polly Scragg, wearing a dirty house dress and wiping a large kitchen knife against her filthy apron. Her enormous tits hung to her waist, no bra hampered them.

From the look, the knife had been cleaner than the apron when she started. Payne hoped they didn't use that on food. He felt bile in his throat.

"Quit foolin' 'round with 'er, Ow. You 'ad your fun last night. S'time to get down to business," she slurred with an almost British accent.

Owen Scragg removed his hands from Susan Sharpe's breasts and moved up toward her head. She gasped but Payne could not see her face.

"Don't worry, Honey," he said to Susan. "The drug is working. You won't feel nuthin'."

The troll of a man moved around to kneel above Susan's head, putting his back to the window Payne saw through, blocking his view. Scragg took the knife from his wife's hand and began to work against the gurgled sounds coming from Susan. All the while Payne could see nothing. But his heart tossed in his chest, knowing whatever was happening just a few feet away could not possibly be good.

160

When Scragg finally moved out of the way, Payne could see the horrible continuity, the fatal circle that completed the story and answered all the open ended questions but still left Payne chilled to his soul. Speechless, motionless, he stood there, watching, waiting…gasping.

Scragg had removed Susan's head with the butcher knife. Now, with a poor imitation of a doctor's precision, he injected something into the neck with large hypos. The body writhed and shuddered but failed to stop moving altogether.

Mrs. Scragg, who had stepped out of the room for the moment, re-entered with a camera in hand. She looked at the image with shock. Sucking in her breath, she spoke condescendingly to her betrothed.

"What the 'ell are you doin'?"

For a moment Payne thought she might run and call the police, even as he should be doing.

"You know you're s'posed to put those in diff-rent places. If you inject in the same spot twice it'll turn black. People don't pay for no black spots, makes it look all fake," she said with a sneer and a little dance.

Mr. Scragg looked up at her then down at his masterpiece of macabre and shrugged like a child who had just been caught painting his school project the wrong color.

"This can be such a pain in the ass sometimes," he growled.

"Yeah," she agreed. "Too bad we can't keep 'em squirmin' for more'n a month."

When thy closes thine eyes against the darkness, keepest thy thoughts pure, for evil lurks ever near. Closer...closer...
Keep the faith, my friends. If that doesn't work, at least keep a flashlight.

Blue Canyon

"Collect the BackSides"

Be sure to check out the fine asses on the back covers.
Each edition has a different ass. Collect them all.

www.songsinthekeyofgoth.webs.com